CALEB BIRCH

PERIL AND SPLENDOR

THE JOURNEY TO YRAGOS

First published 2023
Copyright © 2023 Caleb Birch

ISBN 978-0-6397-5845-9 | Print
ISBN 978-0-6397-5846-6 | Ebook

All editing, design and publishing work completed with love
by the team at: www.myebook.online

Editing by Tracy Buenk
Cover, illustration and interior by Gregg Davies

Dedication

To all the gamers out there.
Keep doing what you love.

CONTENTS

CHAPTER 1

THE LIFE OF WARRIORS

A loud clunk rings through the air as Ramsay blocks a mighty swipe from the Chimera with his shield. Ramsay and his team are in the midst of an intense battle. The Chimera is a terrible beast with the head of a lion, a goat's head on her back, and a snake at the end of her tail. She has already received heavy damage, and her roars echo in the cave as she struggles to fend off the strategic onslaught of Ramsay's team.

"Just a little more!" Ramsay shouts. "Avoid the fire breath and keep attacking."

"Anyone got burns? You guys are making it easy for me," Chase says.

"Ramsay, keep her distracted like that," Eldon shouts.

Eldon swiftly lunges toward the Chimera's flank and thrusts his spear into her side. The Chimera cries out but immediately turns around and hits Eldon away with her claws. Eldon is thrown across the cave and holds on to his spear as it rips out of the creature's side. The claws scratch through Eldon's armor leaving gaping wounds on his arm. Chase casts a spell to heal Eldon while Ramsay rushes the Chimera with a combination of slashes with his sword. He cuts off the snake head just as Jonwido shoots a dark energy ball from his cane and hits the Chimera in the face. Stunned by this attack, the Chimera staggers around disoriented. Ramsay, taking advantage of the situation, runs toward the Chimera and slashes her throat wide open. The vicious beast falls dying to the ground amid the shouts and cheers of victory.

"Eldon, how are you feeling?" Chase asks.

"Can't complain. Your magic still works wonders. I don't have a scratch on me," Eldon responds.

"Okay cool," Chase says.

"Awesome," says Ramsay. "Looks like this beast won't be terrorizing the people of Aegemald any longer. Well done guys."

"There are a lot of skeletons in here. These look like warriors and travelers who were unfortunate enough to meet the Chimera. Let's loot what we can," Jonwido says.

The sunlight is shining through the openings in the ceiling, making it easy for the victorious warriors to search the cave for valuable items on the remains of the Chimera's victims. It's been a long day for our heroes, and now they are about to return to the city to collect their reward.

They leave the Chimera's lair carrying their spoils. Ramsay is chuffed that he has slain another powerful monster. The smile on his face shows it, although he couldn't have done it without his team. He is a veteran knight with considerable experience in monster-hunting missions and at 29 years old, he's already built an impressive reputation in the warriors' guild in the city.

Killing the grisly Chimera is another notch in the belt for him and his team. Jonwido doesn't care much for glory. He is just looking forward to collecting his reward.

AFTER A DAY'S JOURNEY, the team approaches the city of Nashia. This lively city, located in the midst of a beautiful green forest, is their home. They are greeted by the sentries at the main gate as they walk in, and the blood on their armor and garments does not go unnoticed. Ramsay's armor glistens in the afternoon sunlight. He has long gauntlets on his arms, and his feet are enclosed by sabatons that reach up to his knees. Despite the heavy weight of his armor, his strength allows him to be quite nimble when fighting. His duty as a knight is to protect his team. He needs to be heavily armored because all the aggression of the enemies must be directed at him while the rest of the team deals damage.

The wizards in the team are wearing cotton garments. They rarely engage in close combat and need to be as swift as possible. Chase is the white wizard in the team and his duty is healing with magic. Jonwido is the black wizard, and he is responsible for dealing the most damage to enemies.

Eldon wears medium armor and fights mostly in close combat. His spear is covered in coagulated Chimera blood. The group is congratulated and cheered as they walk down the streets. Ramsay receives a few high-fives from acquaintances. The heroes, weary from the journey, head home to rest and get cleaned up.

Later that evening, Ramsay meets up with his friends at The Stoney to celebrate their recent success. The Stoney is a popular tavern where they usually go for drinks. The city is adorned with plenty of trees and greenery, and the tavern has a pleasant view of this from the inside. Ramsay and his comrades are seated at a table near the window.

"That was quite a fearsome monster we beat today. Let's get some drinks to celebrate," Eldon says.

"Yeah, now you're talking. I'm going all in tonight!" Jonwido exclaims.

"I've faced worse monsters than that before, but it was a decent fight," Ramsay says.

"The fire breath and ice breath were an interesting challenge. Fortunately, we avoided most of the nasty attacks," Chase says, as Eldon leaves to get drinks from the bar.

"I hate getting poisoned. Good thing this monster didn't have poison techniques," Ramsay says.

Chase laughs. "Poison is horrible but nothing that a little cure spell won't fix."

"It's a shame to have to kill a creature but sometimes you have to do it for the greater good," Ramsay says.

"You're too nice. That thing was fugly," Jonwido replies.

Eldon returns with the drinks and Jonwido nudges him as he settles back onto his stool.

"Hot girls over there," Jonwido murmurs.

Two curvaceous human girls standing further down the bar are definitely attracting attention in the tavern.

"They are quite pretty," Ramsay responds, glancing surreptitiously in their direction.

"Look, that guy is going to approach them. He seems like a player," Jonwido says.

A tall man, who is casually dressed, approaches one of the girls. He starts chatting with them.

"That guy kind of looks like an asshole," Ramsay says, as he makes a superficial judgement.

"The girls seem to be enjoying their chat with him anyway," Chase says.

"Damn, women are so complicated," Ramsay says.

"When was the last time you had a girlfriend, Ramsay? Eldon asks.

"It's been about a year, I think." Ramsay twists the truth.

"Why have only one girlfriend?" Jonwido jokes.

"Here he goes again. The alcohol appears to be working," Eldon says.

"These dwarves can be real boozers hey," Chase says, as he makes fun of Jon's habit.

Jonwido is a dwarf, and they are known to be heavy drinkers in the realm. There are many different races in the realm of Aegemald. Chase is Elvish, and one can easily recognize this with his pointy ears. Eldon is a regular human, just like Ramsay. He has a positive attitude and a quick smile. Eldon and Ramsay have been friends since they were young.

"You're one of the best knights in the city. How can you still be single?" Eldon asks.

"Hell if I know," Ramsay responds.

Ramsay doesn't say it out loud, but he sometimes feels that doing the right thing can make you miss out on life.

The friends stay till late at The Stoney, having a good time. Some of them have a few too many. The citizens of

Nashia have enjoyed peace for a while now, but there is always work for the teams of the warriors' guild.

A few days pass and Ramsay is at the marketplace browsing for new armor and accessories. It is bustling today and packed with people but there aren't many searching for the same thing as him. The merchants have their stalls set up, side by side, and the goods are laid out for the customers to look at. Ramsay purchases some new gear and a bracelet said to increase its owner's vitality. As he leaves the marketplace and walks down the pathway, a young woman calls to him for help. She is clearly distressed.

"Please help me! You're one of the knights, right? Something bad has happened." The woman is struggling to hold back her tears. "My friends and I were outside the city collecting some plants to study. We are botanists, you see. The three of us were walking and suddenly, these men appeared. They were wearing black robes and looked super weird."

"Then what happened?" Ramsay asks, steering her gently off the busy pathway.

"They attacked us!" she sobs. Brayan struggled, and

they shot him down with their dark magic attacks. They kidnapped Keira! I managed to escape."

"Oh no! I heard rumors of a dark cult that was kidnapping people."

"Please do something," the woman pleads.

"Let me first get my equipment. Then you must take me to the place where this happened."

"Thank you so much," she says, visibly relieved.

"By the way, my name is Ramsay Wick," Ramsay says as they hurry towards the guild armory.

"I'm Octavia," she responds.

RAMSAY COLLECTS his gear while Octavia waits outside the guild. They get Ramsay's horse from the stables and ride together. The location is quite a distance outside the city. The woman shows Ramsay the place where her friends were attacked.

"This is where it happened."

"I see. Let's look around for tracks."

Octavia spots her friend's spectacles. They're twisted and the lenses are broken. Rare flowers are scattered on the ground.

"These are medicinal flowers that my friend was carrying in a bag. We use them to create healing potions.

She must have dropped them in case we came looking for her."

They follow the trail until they reach an entrance to a large, dilapidated building. Occult symbols are painted on the walls in red. Patches of moss cover the corners and edges. They hear long moaning cries coming from inside mixed with ritualistic chanting. The air feels thick and cold, as if nature was depressed.

"This must be their hideout," Ramsay says. "It's not safe here. We must get going."

THE TWO RETURN to the city. Ramsay calls his team members and informs them of what happened. They all live in the same district, which makes it easier for them to gather in case of emergencies. Jonwido slowly comes out of his home as the rest of his team wait for him outside.

"It looks like the dark cult is real and I think I found their hideout," Ramsay says.

"They must be stopped," Chase says. "But we should first report it to the warriors' guild. I'm not doing this for free."

"Oof, I have such a headache," Jonwido says. "Why did you guys let me drink so much?"

Ramsay and the team head for the warriors' guild.

There is a large board with papers pinned to it. Each paper has information about a hunt and the reward for completing it. They go to the reception and ask to speak to the leader. After the report of the dark cult to the leader, it is registered as a mission. With Ramsay on their team, they have more than enough experience and the leader approves the mission. They're named Team Leopadillo.

"All right, is everyone ready for this mission?" Ramsay asks.

"Let me confirm the plan. We invade the base of the dark cult and rescue any captives," Eldon says.

"That's right. At this stage we don't know the strength of the cult or who we'll have to defeat. Be prepared to react quickly. Jon knows the most about dark magic in our group. His expertise might be useful," Ramsay says.

"Cool. Dark magic is all about destructive power. The healer will need to pull up his pristine socks," Jonwido says.

"What was that? I always work hard as a healer. You're always so bloody condescending," Chase says with indignation.

Jonwido burps loudly.

"Enough, guys! We need both of you for this mission," Ramsay says.

OUR HEROES PREPARE themselves for the battle and leave in the morning on horseback. They follow the path Ramsay discovered previously with Octavia.

"I can sense the energetic residue. We are getting close," Chase says as they ride over the creeping vegetation.

"That's right. It's just a little further," Ramsay says.

They arrive at the uninviting entrance to the hideout. No one is standing guard because most would normally run in the opposite direction. Ramsay walks in front and enters the building. Eldon follows closely behind him, and the wizards are at the back of the team. It is quite spacious inside, though very gloomy with demonic statues placed on each side. The team walk quietly down the corridor towards the sound of low voices. The door of the room is slightly ajar, and through the gap, Ramsay sees several cult members wearing long, black robes with cowls. Ramsay unsheathes his sword and takes his shield in his left arm. He signals to the others, and they burst into the room with a roar.

The element of surprise gives the team an advantage and Ramsay slashes at a robed figure with his sword. Jonwido and Eldon begin fighting as well. The other cult members rally quickly and cast dark magic attacks at them, but Chase quickly heals the damage.

Ramsay uses defensive magic to put a protective field around him and draws the attention of the rest of the enemies. He spins around with his sword attacking the enemies surrounding him. They retaliate by casting electric magic attacks at him to inflict paralysis. Ramsay staggers for a few seconds but is unaffected. Jonwido and Eldon have taken down two enemies, and now direct their attacks to the rest of the cult members in the room. Eldon strikes one down with his spear, and Jonwido blasts another one with a fireball. Only one enemy is left standing and Ramsay finishes him with a combination of sword slices.

The team catches their breath and assesses their injuries. Chase casts a regeneration spell and their health starts to slowly recover.

Ramsay looks around the room and spots a body lying on an altar in the corner.

"That could be one of Octavia's friends," he says.

"This confirms the stories about the dark cult abducting and sacrificing people," says Eldon, stepping up for a closer look.

"We must put an end to this madness!" Chase exclaims.

"From the look of the items placed around here, it seems they are trying to resurrect some kind of evil being," Jonwido says.

They leave the room and proceed cautiously down the corridor. Suddenly, what appears to be three skeletons come out of one of the doors and lurch towards Ramsay.

One of them is much bigger than the other two. They screech as they swipe Ramsay with their bony claws. While Ramsay parries their blows, the damage dealers in the team pick them off. The skeletons are surprisingly strong considering that they don't have muscles. After multiple attacks from Eldon and Jonwido, the skeletons begin falling to pieces, until the floor is scattered with ribs and fragments of shattered bone.

After Chase had cast a healing spell, Ramsay continues walking ahead of the team. They reach an elevator with a lever in the middle. Eldon pulls the lever, and thick ropes lift the platform up to the next floor with a mechanical noise. The team arrives by the entrance to a large room as the elevator comes to a stop.

"I feel an intense dark energy coming from this room," Chase says.

"I think they've summoned a demon," Jonwido adds.

"Damn, are you guys ready?" Ramsay says.

It's a little dark inside and there's a platform with another sacrificial altar on it. Loud growls are coming from somewhere in the room. Looking up, Ramsay spots an ugly black creature perched in a space near the ceiling just before it jumps down with a roar and lands in front of him.

"Definitely a demon!" Ramsay shouts as the team braces for an attack.

The hideous quadrupedal creature has two horns on its head, black skin and large teeth, now bared in a snarl.

"Oh shit!" Jonwido exclaims.

Ramsay uses magic to flash a light beam into its eyes to get its attention as Chase casts a spell on the ground to slowly regenerate health over time as they stand in the circular area. Ramsay blocks with his shield as the demon jumps toward him and swipes with its claws. Eldon and Jonwido move quickly behind the demon and attack it; Eldon stabs it, and Jonwido shoots a fireball. The demon's attention is diverted to the damage dealers, and it hits both Jonwido and Eldon with its tail, sending them flying away. Chase casts a healing spell on both of them as they land, mere seconds before the demon turns towards him.

"Oh no, you don't!" Ramsay shouts.

Ramsay lobs his shield at the demon, hitting it right in the head. As the demon whirls towards him, Ramsay casts a magic shield around himself and attacks with an upward slash and then thrusts his sword into its abdomen. The demon's skin is tough and the sword does minimal damage. Eldon swiftly jumps up into the air and lands on the demon's back, piercing it with a thrust of his spear. The demon roars in pain and as it rears up, Eldon falls off. Too late, Ramsay sees it rushing towards him and the savage jaws rip at his arm before he is thrown aside. Ramsay scrabbles in his pocket for the potion and gulps it down, as Jonwido attacks the demon with a lightning bolt. This attack clearly does significant damage to the demon, and with a blood-curdling cry, it leaps to the center of the room.

It begins charging its energy and creates a large purple ball which gets bigger and bigger as electricity flashes around it.

"Everybody watch out!" Ramsay shouts.

There is a huge explosion as the team dives for cover. The demon seems equally disorientated from the blast and amidst the confusion, Eldon staggers forward and stabs it through the head.

The fight is over.

"Well done, Eldon," Ramsay says, breathing heavily, sweat dripping from his chin.

"Cool man, that thing sure kept us on our toes," Eldon responds.

"Let's get out of this creepy place," Ramsay says.

"We haven't looked for any captives in here yet," Eldon says. "Let's see if we can find Octavia's friend."

On the way out, they see a girl wandering around the passageway.

"Hey there, are you okay? Were you kidnapped yesterday?" Ramsay asks.

"Yeah, I'm okay. I thought I was a goner, but then I

heard the fighting and saw you slaughtering these maniacs. Thank you so much."

"Are you the botanist, Kiera?" Eldon asks.

"Yes," the girl replies, confused. "How did you know?"

"You should thank your friend Octavia when we return to the city," Ramsay says.

"I can't wait to get back."

As our heroes leave the building, they witness what appears to be trees that have been burned. Their horses snort because of the smoke in the air. An area of the ground is black with charcoal, and there are smoldering remains of animals. The group stares at the scene, wondering what could've happened.

"What do you think was burnt here?" Eldon asks.

"It could be the aftermath of a battle involving fire magic," Chase speculates.

"Nope. Look on the ground over there. It's glass. No ordinary fire magic could turn the sand into glass like that," Jonwido comments.

"I have a bad feeling about this," says Ramsay. "Let's be on our way."

They arrive safely in the city, and the girl's friends joyfully welcome her back.

Another mission successfully completed by Ramsay and his team.

Chapter 2

A Special Mission

Several days pass and the team find themselves back in the warriors' guild, ready to take on another mission.

"I'd prefer a longer break, but I gotta pay the bills," Jonwido says.

"Yeah, I hear you," replies Ramsay "But remember that there are people who need our help. That other girl would've been sacrificed to a demon had it not been for us."

"I hope the next one doesn't involve another demon," Chase says.

"There's one open mission here that we could look into. The ant people are getting out of hand, and it looks like they want us to defeat the ant king," Ramsay says.

"Why? How could the ant people be much of a problem for us?" Eldon asks.

"They are usually a docile race of beings, but the way things are going, we risk an invasion. Some of them were caught stealing food and crops from us. Their leader is the one to worry about. Instead of going to war, we are going to nip it in the bud and eliminate their leader," Ramsay explains.

"I take it they want to send a small team to infiltrate their colony and kill the king?" Eldon asks.

"Yes, once the king is dead, they will all scatter," Ramsay replies.

"Let's do it," Chase says.

The heroes accept the mission and prepare themselves. Ramsay goes to the market again to replenish his potions and buy a new weapon. A shiny new broadsword catches his eye. It has a blue gemstone in the hilt.

The team meet outside the city gate.

"Nice sword Ramsay," Eldon compliments.

"Thanks. The other one was getting rusty," Ramsay replies.

"The king of the ant people! What does this thing look like?" Jonwido asks.

"He looks like a big ant with razors for arms," Eldon says.

"Where is the base?" Chase asks.

"The entrance to the tunnel system is in the mountain of the giants, near the ancient ruins," Ramsay answers.

There is no risk of running into any giants because they haven't been seen there in ages.

Ramsay and the team follow the route to their destination. The surroundings are mountainous with big rocks scattered around, and the path on which they travel is grassy. About halfway there, they spot a man standing on the side of the road. He is scraggy and is dressed like a merchant. He waves to the group to stop and explains to Ramsay that he witnessed people being ambushed by ogres.

"Good sir, you must follow me! I will take you to the spot where I saw the ogres. You must stop them from harming any more innocent victims," the man requests urgently.

"All right, lead the way. We'll put an end to the murderous ogres," Ramsay responds.

"We've got the time for a little detour, and might as well sort this out while we're here. Is everyone with me?" Ramsay asks the team.

"Yeah, I'm good with it," Eldon responds.

"When are you going to say no to these people? Jonwido says, crossly "I'm not turning back alone, but this doesn't mean I like it."

"Let's go get this done," Chase says.

The man leads them to the opening of a narrow path through the mountain. He says that the ogres are camping on the other side. It looks very uninviting. They begin to proceed in single file down the path with a rocky wall looming high on each side. Suddenly, the man runs ahead and disappears into a crevice as darts begin raining down. Eldon, Chase, and Jonwido are hit with multiple shots and as their legs begin to buckle beneath them, they realize the darts have been coated with a strong tranquilizer. The darts bounce off Ramsay's metal body armor as his friends drop to the ground and fall unconscious.

"Damn, this was a trap! You tricky bastard!" Ramsay shouts.

Several bandits drop down from above. They were clearly waiting for their targets to pass through this spot. They are wielding curved swords and Ramsay knows it would be difficult to dispatch all these enemies by himself. He glances helplessly at his friends lying on the ground.

To his surprise, more arrows rain down and some of the bandits drop. A slender, yet strong female figure appears, holding a bow. She aims it at the rest of them, pulling the bowstring back tightly, and shoots multiple arrows at once. It appears that she uses magic too since the arrows are lit up with a flame. The bandits fall and lie motionless, apparently wiped out. Three others join her where she stands. Ramsay approaches them.

"You're lucky we were in the area," the woman says.

"That was a nasty ambush. We saw them waiting at the top of this chasm."

"Yeah, thanks for the help. Could you heal my friends please?" Ramsay asks.

One of them walks over to Ramsay's three friends and a white aura surrounds them before they wake up, dazed. It seems she is a mage. Ramsay informs his friends of what had happened.

"You guys are also part of the warrior's guild. It's nice to finally meet you. I'm Ramsay."

"Likewise. I'm Irina. These are my teammates, Romulus, Verdan, and Phinara," the woman responds as she flicks back her raven hair.

"We all know who you are, Ramsay," Romulus says.

"Ah, looks like my reputation precedes me," Ramsay says.

"Thanks for healing us, Phinara," Chase says.

"You're welcome."

"You guys out on a mission?" Eldon asks.

"Yes, we're on our way to kill a monster," Irina replies.

"All right, travel safely. We can handle ourselves now," Ramsay says. "Bye."

"Bye," Irina says with a smile.

The teams turn to leave, but when Ramsay glances back, Irina's cool green eyes are still fixed on him.

"My bad, guys. I got us into a trap," Ramsay says to his team as the sun begins to fade.

"Shit happens. We're lucky that her team was here to help," Eldon says.

"Next time don't be so gullible, Ramsay," Jonwido remarks.

"We're okay now. It's getting late. We best look for a place to camp for the night," Chase advises.

"Did you see how pretty Irina is?" Eldon asks.

"Yeah, she's nice," Ramsay replies awkwardly.

Ramsay's team sets up a camp nearby and rests for the night. At sunrise, they get ready to continue their journey to the main hive of the ant people. However, before setting off, they notice something alarming.

"Everyone, look at the sky over there," Chase says.

"It's a cloud of smoke, and it's exactly in the direction of Nashia!" Eldon exclaims.

"Yeah, that's not good," Ramsay says.

"It looks like a huge fire," Jonwido says.

"Let's head back to the city. We must see what's happening," Ramsay says.

Hurriedly packing the last saddlebag, they mount their horses and gallop back to the city. As they approach, they see a large grey dragon flying in the sky above. It descends and blasts the people and buildings with its fiery breath. Their horses stop abruptly, wide-eyed and whinnying in fear, as our heroes look on in amazement.

"Seven hells! This can't be happening!" Ramsay exclaims.

The team is awestruck by the sight. They look at each other as their minds race to decide on what to do first.

"Guys, hold yourselves together! We must save as many as we can. Chase, protective and healing barriers! Don't engage the dragons! We don't know what we're up against," Ramsay commands.

Three huge dragons are destroying parts of the city, burning structures, and devouring people and animals. Blood and charcoal are seen all around. The knights and warriors of the city try their best to defend the people, but the lack of preparation and chaos make their efforts ineffective. It is truly a disaster. The white mages heal as many as they can. Archers fire arrows at the dragons. Others are being saved from burning buildings and taken to safety.

After what feels like an eternity, the dragons lose interest and leave to return to their nests. People start picking up the pieces and recovering their loved ones. Women and children cry in the streets. It is a terrible day in the city of Nashia.

After a period of respite, the king gathers the people together to give a speech and hold a memorial ceremony for the victims of the dragon onslaught. The people clearly fear that the dragons will return. The king's army immediately begins building up the defenses of the city, and the scholars study what they can about the dragons to determine how best to fight them. The warriors' guild has a more adventurous duty. They must plan to put an end to the dragon scourge once and for all.

Ramsay hears that an important meeting is to be held at the warriors' guild, and all members are invited. The purpose of the meeting is to discuss the most important mission in the history of the guild: To defeat the dragons. When Team Leopadillo arrives at the venue it's already packed, and the air is filled with conversations. Irina and her team are at the meeting too. Like Ramsay, they arrived late at the scene when the dragons attacked. Those in attendance are waiting in anticipation for what is going to be said. Some consider this to be a suicide mission, whereas others are excited about the opportunity to test their strength on an S-rank mission.

"This is going to be interesting. It's a historical moment for the guild," Chase says.

"There are many powerful members here. How many will remain?" Ramsay asks a rhetorical question.

"I'm ready to make those flying lizards pay for what they've done," Eldon says.

Jonwido remains silent.

"Jonwido, my condolences to your family," Ramsay says.

"Sorry for the loss, man," Eldon adds.

Jonwido's family had been killed in the incident, including his parents.

The guild leader, Seth, steps up to the podium, and everyone becomes quiet. With a serious tone, he begins to speak.

"Welcome friends. The city of Nashia was founded 500 years ago. Since then, we have enjoyed peace in this fertile land. The warriors' guild has protected this place from vicious, powerful monsters. A couple of weeks ago this city was attacked by dragons. Our families and comrades were slaughtered. It was a massacre that is unknown in our history. Dragons are wild beasts, but they are intelligent. These creatures live for thousands of years. They came to fill their bellies and destroy our home.

"Our wisest scholars tell us that dragons come out of their hidden world every 2160 years. This time has come, and we must prepare.

"You have been called here for a purpose; to go to the heart of the dragons and kill their alpha leader. Our scouts have located the region where the dragons are coming from. The journey will be perilous. You will have to face the most dangerous enemies. You are here for your families! You are here for your honor!"

Most of the members respond together by shouting and cheering.

The guildmaster continues, "What has happened must not happen again. I have no doubt that there are people in this room who are more than capable of defeating the alpha. Rest assured that the reward will be grand. The king himself will bestow great honor upon those who are victorious. Only teams of four will qualify to officially be assigned on this mission."

"Are we all committed to this mission?" Ramsay asks his team.

"Do you need to ask?" Eldon replies with a grin.

"I'm in," Chase responds.

"Of course," Jonwido responds.

After much deliberation, the teams present make their decision. Six teams remain to accept the mission. The twenty-four individuals standing in the room represent the cream of the crop. Standing among them is Kharis, a bloodthirsty berserker. He lays waste on the battlefield with his mighty axe. From the East, there is Danjurou. Facing him is like walking into a whirlwind of samurai blades. Elyon is one of the best gunslingers in the realm. He uses his pistols to quickly fill his targets with holes.

Vaeril and Qamara are noteworthy dark mages. And of course, Ramsay is the pre-eminent knight of the city.

A FEW DAYS later we find Ramsay tossing in his bed, struggling to fall asleep. He feels a burden weighing heavily on him. His room is well-decorated and very neat. There is a desk with some philosophical and magical books stacked on it and a pair of chairs. Several trophies are displayed on a cabinet and a sword is leaning against it. The curtains bulge and recede slowly as the wind comes in through the open window.

Does everyone expect me to defeat the dragon alpha? he thinks.

What if I fail, and more people get killed.

THE NEXT DAY, Ramsay is in a gloomy mood. He takes a walk to the city canal. The place is surrounded by flowers and beautiful trees and many city folks come here to relax. The sunshine glitters on the water. A hawk flies down towards him and he recognizes it as one of his old teacher's hawks. It lands on his arm, and he removes the paper from the bird's leg. It is an invitation from Galather, his teacher.

He wants to share some wisdom for the upcoming adventure. Ramsay owes all his training in defensive magic to this renowned mage. Ramsay puts the letter in his pocket and sits on the bench nearby to ponder.

Eldon, Chase, and Jonwido are preparing themselves in their own way.

CHAPTER 3

A HOP TO THE DESERT

It is close to sunset in Nashia and Ramsay walks to Galather's house. The garden in front is well cared for; bushes and trees are neatly pruned. He makes his way up to the open front door where a black cat is sitting on a comfortable chair near the entrance.

"Master is inside. He has been waiting for you," the cat says.

"Okay Seto," Ramsay replies and pets the cat.

Most people would be disturbed by the talking cat, but Ramsay is used to it. Galather appears at the door wearing a black silk robe with black feathers at the back of his shoulders. Crystal necklaces on his chest peek out through his long grey beard.

"Ramsay, it has been long. Come inside."

Ramsay follows Galather to a room with strange and interesting items placed around.

"You have a great adventure ahead of you. Do you have the resolve to see it through?" Galather asks.

"I'm not sure. I recently got my team into trouble and almost cost them their lives. This was all because I was too naïve. I was eager to help someone and got led into an ambush. This time I must lead my team into a far more dangerous situation."

"You have a good heart. That's what makes you strong. Believe in yourself."

"I fear the people are looking to me to save them from the dragons. It is a heavy burden."

"You may be the top knight in the city, but you're not on everyone's mind. Don't be afraid to seek help from your comrades. Also, I have something for you which may help you to accomplish your mission."

Galather opens a chest on the table. He reaches inside and takes out a green crystal ball with engravings on it.

"Wow, what is it?" Ramsay asks.

"This is a dragon shackle orb. Hold it up and say the incantation, and a dragon will be drained of all his energy. Use it on the alpha. This will give you the chance to deliver the death blow. It is extremely rare. Legend has it, that if the orb contains enough energy, it will also allow its owner to make one wish. However, no one knows how long it can hold the energy. Use it wisely."

"Amazing. This gift is invaluable. This will give us a fighting chance."

Galather hands Ramsay a paper with writing on it.

"Memorize this incantation."

"I will," says Ramsay as he looks at the aged paper.

Ramsay puts the orb and paper in a bag.

"As to the exact location of the alpha dragon's lair, I cannot tell you. You'll need to journey to the region where the dragons were last spotted and find clues. When you face challenges, do what you decide to do, but remember that you cannot decide what you will decide to do. That you must do when the moment comes. Be strong."

"Thanks for the wise words, Master. My spirits have been uplifted."

"I have a message for Eldon as well. He has great potential for dragon slaying. He needs to learn to jump."

"All right, I'll let him know."

Ramsay leaves the house with fire in his eyes and ready to go out on the adventure. Training and preparation would benefit our heroes now, but it is urgent that they leave early in the morning.

The dragons might return at any time.

As the sun is rising, Ramsay and his team meet near the northern city gates. Their horses are packed with supplies and equipment. A small crowd has gathered to send them off. Renovations are being done on the buildings around them to repair the damage caused by the dragons. There are areas that still appear scorched. It is clear what the heroes are up against. The people cheer and clap as they go on their way.

The team is trotting along a path through the woods on their horses. Chase has the map.

"You know where we are going first?" Eldon asks.

"Our first stop is the city of Ilaburn. It's about three days of traveling to the north. The guild let us know that the dragons were last spotted in the land of Yragos. As it is quite far away, I suggest we rest for a few days at each city along the way," Chase answers.

"Yep, I like that idea," Jonwido says.

"What is it like in Ilaburn?" Ramsay asks.

"It's a hot, desert environment. You're going to miss Nashia. Trust me," Chase responds.

"Yeah, you're going to die in that armor, Ramsay," Eldon says.

Ramsay shrugs.

"Jonwido is dressed perfectly for this," Eldon says.

Jonwido is wearing a silk robe and pointed mage hat. This definitely looks cooler.

"Lucky me," Jonwido says.

"Nashia is most likely not the only city that has been attacked," Ramsay says.

"The other cities would've been helpless too," Eldon adds.

"Nashia was probably their prime target though. If I were a dragon, I would choose to feast in a lush city with water and ample people and animals. Ilaburn is nothing like it," Chase says.

They stop the horses for a moment to refill their water canteens at a stream and let the horses drink.

Ramsay takes the dragon shackle orb out of his saddlebag and unwraps it carefully. He holds the green globe towards the others, and they step closer to inspect it.

"Is that what I think it is? Impossible!" Jonwido exclaims, astonished.

"I met up with my old master. He gave me this dragon shackle orb and said we should use it on the alpha," Ramsay explains.

"We might be able to kill this thing after all. I assume he gave you the incantation as well," Jonwido comments.

"Yeah, got it right here," Ramsay replies.

"Let's not lose the orb," Jonwido says.

"Galather had a message for you too, Eldon. He said that you need to learn to jump, and that you have great potential as a dragon slayer," Ramsay says.

"Oh, he was referring to the legend of the ancient dragon hunters. They wielded spears and were able to jump high enough to land on a dragon's back and impale it. I will need to train harder to gain such abilities," Eldon responds.

"You are already proficient with a spear. That's a start," Chase says.

The group starts moving again. As the day nears its end, they come to a shady oak tree next to the steep side of a hill. They haven't seen any predators in this area and the ground is mostly level.

"This looks like a good spot to set up camp," Chase says.

"Where's the cooking pot, I'm feeling famished, "Eldon says.

Eldon starts preparing a fire. After eating, they talk for a while and get ready to sleep. Ramsay sits on his blanket turning the shackle orb in his hand. The light of the campfire moves in the translucent orb.

What a beautiful thing, Ramsay thinks.

He puts it in the bag next to him and falls asleep.

NEAR DAYBREAK, a creature enters the camp while the four warriors are sleeping. His small footsteps are too soft to be heard. The creature searches their bags and items for valuables. He picks up the bag next to Ramsay and takes the shackle orb out.

Wow, the creature thinks. *This ball is so nice.*

Ramsay wakes up and sees a black rabbit, standing on two legs, and holding the orb. It's about the same height as a dwarf. He stares for a moment trying to figure out if it's a dream.

"Hey give that back!" Ramsay shouts.

"Ahhh!" the rabbit screams and scurries away with the orb.

Ramsay throws the blanket off and jumps up as the rest of the team wakes up from the noise.

"Everyone get up! A rabbit just stole the shackle orb! I'm going after it," Ramsay says, grabbing his sword.

"What? A rabbit?" Chase asks.

They all look at each other with bewildered expressions.

"Yes, a freaking rabbit, come!" Ramsay says as he runs after the rabbit, leaving his outer armor behind.

Chase and Jonwido get up immediately and follow in pursuit, but Eldon stays behind to look after the horses and supplies. They chase the rabbit, jumping over rocks and sliding on the ground. Ramsay can barely keep up. The rabbit makes a sharp turn, and Ramsay trips and falls onto the sandy ground. He curses, quickly stands up, and continues the chase with the rest of the group following closely behind. The rabbit darts into an open area and jumps onto some boulders, and then up onto the high ground. There are huts and structures around the area. He looks down as Ramsay approaches.

"I'm going to chase you down. You'll be sorry when I catch you. You'd better give it back now!" Ramsay shouts.

"This is my shiny ball now!" The rabbit answers and taunts him with the orb.

"You talk?" Ramsay shouts in surprise.

Chase and Jonwido catch up and stand by Ramsay's side. Ogres start coming out of the huts. Ramsay realizes that the rabbit has led them into an ogre village. The ogres are tall and bulky and have large protruding teeth. They have green skin with hair covering their arms and back. Ogres are also aggressive and are known to be fond of eating infants.

A dozen ogres surround Ramsay and his friends. One of the ogres walks closer to them.

"What do we have here? Some strangers have come into our village. Give us the child," the ogre says.

"What child?" Ramsay asks, bewildered until he follows the ogre's focused stare.

"I'm not a child, you smelly imbecile!" Jonwido says angrily.

"Heheheh," the ogre chuckles.

"I've had enough!" Jonwido exclaims.

Jonwido raises his staff and says an incantation. His eyes start to glow as lightning descends from the sky and strikes the ogres in the vicinity. Chase and Ramsay shield their eyes from the bright flashes with their arms. After a thunderous noise, the ogres lay dead around them, smoking.

"Wow, he is so strong!" the rabbit exclaims in awe, and its eyes bulge.

A couple more ogres approach Ramsay, swinging their clubs, but Ramsay dispatches them quickly with his sword.

"Damn, we didn't come here to kill these ogres," Ramsay says with remorse.

Suddenly, an ogre appears behind the rabbit and picks him up by the long ears.

"Ye'll make a nice stew rabbit. What are ye holding there?" the ogre asks as he looks at the orb.

"Put the rabbit down, or you'll end up like your friends here," Ramsay says.

The ogre hesitates with a scowl before throwing the rabbit down to Ramsay, and backing into the woods.

"Here, take the orb. Just don't hurt me. Please!" the rabbit begs.

Ramsay picks up the shackle orb.

"What kind of rabbit are you? How can you speak?" Chase asks.

"Ah, I'm not a normal rabbit. Yep," the rabbit says, smiling.

"My name is Peakiboon, and I'm an Ulua rabbit. We Ulua are more evolved than the small ones you know of. Yep. We can speak and do many things."

"Interesting," Ramsay says. "But you have wasted our time and we need to go now."

They turn to go back to the campsite.

"Wait, can I come with you?" Peakiboon asks.

"No, we are on a dangerous mission," Ramsay says. "And you're a thief. Why would we let you join us?"

"I don't care about the danger. I'm brave and useful. Yep. You'll see. Please. Please," the rabbit persists, trailing behind the team as they head back to camp.

Ramsay ignores the rabbit for a while but eventually gives in.

"Okay okay, you can join us if you don't slow us down. And don't touch the orb," Ramsay says finally.

"Yep. Gotcha, gotcha. I will be good," Peakiboon agrees.

"Do your part to help us get food, or Jonwido here might decide to cook a roast rabbit," Ramsay jokes.

The rabbit gulps nervously.

The group returns to the camp to find Eldon pacing anxiously.

"Have you got the orb? And why have you guys brought the rabbit back?" Eldon asks.

"Hello, Peakiboon is my name," the rabbit says.

"It talks?" Eldon exclaims, surprised.

"Yeah, a bit too much if you ask me," Ramsay adds.

They prepare to continue their journey towards Ilaburn and mount their horses. The rabbit rides together with Ramsay. They leave the forest, and the environment starts becoming sandier. The land is strewn with jagged rocks and parts of ancient statues and ruins. There are no trees around now, but small bushes are scattered over the ground. It is sunny and warm, and the team rides along the path. They stop in their tracks as a gigantic scorpion appears at the top of a ridge and crawls down onto the path in front of them. The scorpion is much larger than a horse and its tail lifts about ten feet into the air. It raises its black pincers and screeches loudly.

Peakiboon slips off Ramsay's horse with a scream and scurries behind a large rock.

"Woh, that's a huge scorpion," Ramsay says.

They dismount, and the horses back away nervously behind a rocky outcrop. Ramsay walks towards the scorpion, holding his shield out as the scorpion comes at him. It attacks a couple of times with its pincers, but Ramsay blocks them with his shield, keeping it busy while Eldon moves to its flank. Eldon dashes towards it, jumps up, and strikes its back with the spear. The spear penetrates a weak spot in its hard outer shell and kills it.

"There, nice strike," Ramsay says.

"Don't celebrate yet," Chase says, as two more large scorpions appear and crawl toward them. Ramsay fights the one, and the rest of the team deals with the other one. Peakiboon remains hidden and watches the battle from a distance. Jonwido shoots fireballs at the scorpion and dodges a pincer attack. Eldon attacks the legs, breaking some of them. The scorpion rotates and thrusts Eldon with its tail, stabbing him with the barb. Chase realizes that Eldon has been poisoned and quickly performs a cure spell. Jonwido casts a spell, and his staff turns into a sword of light. He cuts the scorpion's tail off, and slices through the shell. It falls flat on the ground. Eldon lies on his back, recovering from the poisonous wound. Chase is standing over him with his hands out.

Ramsay is still engaged in combat with his scorpion foe. It tries to thrust its tail at him, but he dodges and cuts the barb off. A green liquid sprays out of the tail. Ramsay performs another combo, swinging a few times horizontally, turning around, with a final thrust, plunges his sword into the scorpion's head.

The fight is over.

Peakiboon hops out from behind the rock, goes to one of the scorpions, and starts punching it with jabs and straights. He thinks it's dead, but the scorpion moves a little. Peakiboon screams again and jumps away. The group laughs.

"Haha, I think it's dead now, Peakiboon," Eldon laughs.

"You're a strong bunch. Yep. Very strong! Those scorpions looked like they wanted to eat me. Everyone wants to eat me!" Peakiboon says.

THE FOLLOWING DAY, the team travels across the rocky landscape, crossing bridges and riding over dunes until they reach a place from where the city of Ilaburn can be seen. Cacti and elephant trees decorate the desert landscape. An enormous stone stairway lies in front of the eastern city gate. High stone walls prevent anyone standing outside from seeing the city. Ramsay and his team ride up a flat section of the stairway made for horses. They pass the guards and enter the city.

Unlike Nashia, there are no trees and lush vegetation in between the houses and structures, but these are impressive buildings with intricate architecture. The roads are paved with beautiful cobblestone patterns. It is late afternoon, and Ramsay and his team deposit their horses at the stables near the entrance.

"This place is big," Ramsay says.

"The buildings are magnificent," Chase says.

"I know this city. I was here a few times. Yep," Peakiboon says.

"Good, we'll ask you if we get lost," Ramsay says.

"I can't wait to have a jug of ale. Let's go to the closest tavern," Eldon says.

"Yes, I want to fill my belly," Jonwido adds.

"This way! This way!" Peakiboon leads.

They walk down the street, passing the markets. It is bustling with people. There are fire dancers performing on the side of the street and people gathering to watch. Most people are dressed in cotton tunics with beautiful embroidery and headdresses.

Shady-looking characters standing in a corner watch the team as they walk by. Ramsay and his friends don't look like they're from around here. People also turn to look at the big rabbit.

"We kind of stand out in the crowd, don't we?" Chase says.

"I need to make a turn by the markets later for some new weapons and gear," Eldon says.

"Yeah, good idea," Ramsay responds.

"Here it is. Yep. The tavern," Peakiboon points out.

The group enters the tavern, called the Thirsty Camel, and look around for a table to seat them all. They split up and go to different tables since there are no open tables to seat all five of them. Three local men approach Ramsay and Eldon.

"That's some nice armor you have on. You lot traveling from far? What brings you to Ilaburn?" one of the men asks.

"We're on our way to Yragos and had to stop here. We're looking for the dragons," Ramsay answers.

"Oh, you have a long way ahead of you. That's very brave. We heard that they have begun terrorizing the realm."

"They attacked Nashia, where we're from. We're going to make sure it doesn't happen again," Eldon says.

"They obviously haven't been here in Ilaburn," Ramsay says.

"Well, may the gods be with ya. All of us would just run for our lives if the dragons showed up. Be careful here though. Very few can be trusted," the local man says.

"What do you mean?" Ramsay asks.

"Ilaburn can be a rough place. Some people would do anything for some coin," the man responds.

"Let's order something to eat," Eldon says.

Our warriors enjoy a good meal and some ale. The roasted meat is delicious.

"Hey, look who's here," Eldon says, pointing.

Ramsay turns around to look as Irina and her team enter the tavern. Her long, dark hair is unmistakable.

"You got to go talk to her man," Eldon suggests.

"Hmm, yeah, but shouldn't I give them a chance to settle down first?" Ramsay asks.

"Just go, man," Eldon insists.

Ramsay walks up to Irina and greets her.

"Hi, Irina. How was the trip?"

"Hi Ramsay, we made the journey without getting into any danger. We arrived here yesterday," Irina responds.

"That's good. We just got here today. Traveling here wasn't so smooth though. Had to battle some giant scorpions, but here we are."

"Wow, glad you made it."

Irina's teammates go to the front to get drinks and leave them to talk.

"We have a new friend on our team. You see that big rabbit over there?" Ramsay says.

"It's so cute," Irina says.

"I caught him trying to steal something from us. He tried to run for it, but after he was caught, he wanted to come with us."

"Was it something valuable he wanted?"

"Yeah, we have a dragon shackle orb that will help us defeat the alpha. I don't want everyone to see it."

"Wow, how does it work?"

"My master told me that it can drain a dragon of all its energy when used with an incantation. It may be used to grant a wish as well."

"That's amazing. It'll give you a huge advantage."

After a few hours of chatting and flirting, he leaves the tavern with Irina, and they walk the streets of Ilaburn. Although it's getting late, there are still many people out.

"I want to say thanks again for saving me that other time. My team was almost injured because of me," Ramsay says as he takes her hand.

"You're welcome. I don't think the dragons will be defeated by someone like me. I just hope my team will be able to assist those who are capable. That's why we're on this mission. I believe you can do it," Irina says.

"Thanks, it means a lot," Ramsay replies.

Ramsay and Irina enjoy each other's conversation and laugh as they walk back to the inn where both teams are staying. Irina has had a crush on Ramsay for a while, but he has always seemed aloof and preoccupied when in the guild. She is finally getting to know him on a deeper level. This time is precious since either of them might die on the mission. Romance sparks between them and they decide to spend the night together. The next morning, they get ready for the new day.

"Last night was amazing," Ramsay says.

"Yes, it was," Irina says.

"I hope we'll meet again soon on our way to Yragos."

"May we meet again soon. Here take this linkshard," she says, slipping the tiny cone-shaped piece of enchanted quartz into his hand "You'll be able to contact me with it."

"Take care. Bye."

They kiss and part ways outside the Inn. Ramsay is in a great mood today. He starts walking to the tavern to find his team. On the way there, outside a jewelry store, he hears a commotion going on and someone shouting for help. One of the denizens is lying on the hot sidewalk, getting kicked by a big man in leather clothing. He is being mugged. Three more thugs are standing there. Other people witness the situation but turn around and leave as soon as they realize what's happening.

"I already gave you all I have. Please!" the man on the ground pleads.

"You best shut up boy!" the thug shouts.

"Let him go," Ramsay says, approaching the group.

The thugs turn and glare at him. The main thug is alerted to the shiny armor that Ramsay has on and looks at his gang. There are four of them against Ramsay.

"Are you stupid or something, Tin Can? Piss off!" the main thug threatens.

Ramsay unsheathes his sword and raises his shield and slowly starts walking toward the group. He feels fired up with indignation. This is the kind of problem Ramsay is passionate about.

"Hahaha, you must be new around here. There are no heroes in this place. Let's teach him a lesson, boys," the thug says.

One of the thugs holds a spear, one wields a curved sword, another takes out a grimoire, and the leader unsheathes his sword. It is clear that they are hardened criminals. One tries to slice Ramsay's face with the sword, but he parries and kicks him away. The thug with the spear gets close and attempts to thrust at Ramsay. Ramsay dodges to the side and bashes him with the shield so that he falls. Ramsay then moves around the space, keeping his enemies in front of him. The man with the grimoire casts a spell with it and fires dark energy balls at Ramsay, who blocks them with his shield.

The victim gets up and runs away quickly, picking up his satchel. Ramsay casts a defensive spell on himself to negate the damage from the dark magic. A white light cloaks Ramsay for a moment. The thugs with the spear and curved sword make another attempt at attacking Ramsay. Ramsay does an area attack by jumping up and hitting his sword into the ground when landing. The circular area around him lights up and beams of light shoot up out of the ground knocking the men backward. The mage thug fires more dark energy attacks at Ramsay, but they cause no damage because of the magic negation spell Ramsay cast earlier. They are confounded by Ramsay's abilities and stand panting and confused.

"I'm on a mission to kill much more formidable enemies than you pitiful thugs," Ramsay says.

The main thug charges at Ramsay wildly, swinging his sword. The clanging sound of their swords draws spectators as they fight. After blocking the main thug's attacks, Ramsay hits his sword away and slashes his leg. He cries out as he falls to his knees and Ramsay turns his gaze to the others.

"You want more? Get out of here!" Ramsay shouts.

They flinch and start making their escape, helping their leader limp away. The small group gathered a short distance away clap at Ramsay's performance.

Ramsay waves back at them and continues on his way to meet up with his friends, feeling the warm glow of satisfaction at their appreciation.

The sun is bright in the sky, and it is getting hot outdoors. Ramsay finds Chase, Jonwido, and Peakiboon waiting in a shaded area near the Thirsty Camel. Apparently, Chase and Jonwido have been arguing again, judging by their scowls.

"Ramsay! You're back!" Peakiboon greets.

"Hi Peakiboon," Ramsay responds.

"Who was that woman you were talking to last night?" Peakiboon asks.

"She's, uh, a new friend. It's none of your business," Ramsay says.

"Ah Ramsay, I've searched around for information about where we should journey next. I think the best way forward is to find the old railway to the north of the city and follow it across the desert until we reach some green jungle forests. Then we should travel to the gulf of Niparey, where we will need to take a ship across the waters. Jonwido disagrees," Chase says.

"The desert is hot, and I don't like sailing over the ocean!" Jonwido exclaims.

"It's safer and easier to navigate than going through the mountains," Chase argues.

"Whatever, Whitey," Jonwido says.

"I don't like traveling in the heat of the desert, but Chase has a point. Where is Eldon?" Ramsay asks.

"He was training his jumping when we left him by the statue," Chase says.

Near the eastern gate is a statue of the Sultan of Ilaburn that overlooks the open street. There are stairways on either side of it. Eldon is practicing by jumping from the sidewalk up onto the floor by the statue. He jumps up but only manages to grab onto the edge. After dozens of tries, he successfully lands at the top. He needs to jump higher than that to slay dragons. Ramsay and the others arrive, and Eldon greets them from above.

"Hey, Eldon! You managed to jump up there. Nice!" Ramsay says.

"Yeah, finally got it right!" Eldon responds.

Peakiboon runs and effortlessly jumps up to Eldon.

"Me too!" Peakiboon says.

"What? You made that look so easy," Eldon says with his mouth hanging open.

The group laughs, and Eldon and Peakiboon walk down to the ground level.

"Let's go to the marketplace to get new equipment for the next part of the journey," Ramsay says.

The team makes a turn in the marketplace. Eldon buys a new spear for himself and a headdress for the sun. The spear has a large blade with a slight curve in the front. Chase gets himself a new pair of hose and a new healing necklace and bracelet. Jonwido's eye catches a well-embellished staff with greater power than the one he has. Ramsay purchases a new chest cuirass and gauntlets which have a slight blue hue, and a hat. Eldon also buys some carrots for Peakiboon.

"How did it go with Irina last night?" Eldon asks Ramsay on the side.

"It went well, bro. I crushed it," Ramsay says, grinning.

"Awesome, you're the man," Eldon says.

Our heroes make their way to the stables, just a short distance along the stained cobblestone pavements. The sun shines brightly against the stone walls of the buildings above them. Ramsay and the others collect their horses. Ramsay's horse is named Rebel. They pack their new purchases into their bags and make sure they have all their belongings. Ramsay looks for the dragon shackle orb but can't find it. He panics for a moment.

"Has anyone seen the shackle orb?" Ramsay asks.

The rest of his team shrug and look at him with blank faces. None of them know where it is.

"Oh, I have it here. Yep, hehe." Peakiboon has pulled a prank and reveals the orb.

"Seven hells, Peakiboon! Give it here," Ramsay commands, annoyed. "That's not funny. If we run out of food, I know whom we can eat."

Peakiboon gulps and looks chastened.

Finally ready, they proceed to the northern city gate and set out in the direction of the old Ilaburn railway track.

CHAPTER 4

FIERY AVENGER

Ramsay and his team gallop through the desert with determination, looking for the railway. The faster they ride, the less time they need to spend in the heat.

"There! I see it. The old railway," Chase says.

They reach the railway and start riding along it. The environment is a hot, rugged desert. Huge rocky arcs can be seen towering above them. The team keeps riding and approaching a canyon, where the railway passes over a bridge. They cross over, enjoying the beautiful view despite sweating in the high temperature.

"I can't wait till we're out of this desert," Ramsay says.

"Not too far now," Chase says.

As they enter another stretch of desert, suddenly, a large shadow appears over them. As it moves over the sand, they recognize what it is.

"Dragon!" Eldon shouts.

Woosh! The dragon circles them as it gets closer.

"Incoming!" Ramsay shouts.

The shackle orb pulses brightly in Ramsay's bag. Ramsay and his team leap from their horses as they withdraw their weapons, except for Peakiboon, who screams and hops behind a cactus. The dragon lands in front of them with a screeching roar, creating a violent windstorm with its wings. Its large horns extend backward from its head and its gleaming eyes are fixed on its intended victims.

"SHROARRGH!!! The dragon roars.

Ramsay darts forward to attack, but the dragon breathes fire from right to left in a sweeping motion. Ramsay is caught in the flames and receives burn injuries. The others dodge the flames just in time. Chase immediately casts a barrier around each of them to reduce damage, and then a large healing circle on the ground to regenerate their health slowly as they stand in it. Ramsay casts his defensive magic barrier and then charges at the dragon again. He strikes its chest and leg, and it counters by swiping with its large claw. Ramsay blocks with his shield but is thrown backward.

Eldon also gets close and thrusts at the dragon with his spear but can't manage to get a hit. The dragon moves too wildly and erratically. He needs to dodge the claws and stay on his feet. Jonwido stands further away and fires electric balls of energy at the dragon. *Zap! Zap!* The dragon takes a small amount of damage from the energy balls. It roars and fires a short burst of flames in a wide area in front of it as it lurches up into flight. The flames singe all four of them as they try desperately to duck out of range.

"Watch out, here he comes!" Ramsay shouts.

The dragon banks in the sky, and then dives straight at Ramsay, knocking him off his feet. It rises again, circles around, and comes in for another attack, this time aiming for Eldon. He jumps up as it comes in, attempting to hit it in the back but his jump is not high enough and he's slammed by one of the wings. Eldon falls to the ground as the dragon flies up again preparing for another diving attack. This time the dragon is aiming for Chase. Jonwido points his staff at one of the large boulders in the area and uses gravity magic to lift it and shoot it at the dragon. The boulder flies close to the dragon but misses. As the dragon swoops down, Chase casts a wind spell and blows the dragon upwards with a small tornado.

As the creature spirals up into the sky, he uses the break to heal Ramsay and Eldon.

"How are we going to beat this dragon?" Eldon shouts.

"Just keep wearing it down! That's all I can think of!" Ramsay shouts in reply.

The dragon circles and swoops down a few more

times, throwing fire down at Ramsay and his team. They dodge and roll out of the way. Chase heals their burns in between.

"We can't keep this up forever!" Chase shouts.

The dragon descends again for another diving attack, but Jonwido casts an ice spell and shoots ice shards and hail at it.

"Blizzard! Take that!" Jonwido shouts.

This seems to be more effective. The dragon roars as it falls and smashes into the ground.

Ramsay runs toward the dragon, which is getting onto its feet, despite its injuries. Ramsay slices it with sword combos while dodging its bites and scratches. His armor is damaged with holes and dents. It knocks Ramsay back again. Eldon also engages it and gets in a stab before being hit away with the tail.

Jonwido attacks from the side with a gust of freezing wind and ice shards. The battle continues for a painfully long time, with Ramsay and Eldon fighting the dragon from the front while Jonwido attacks it with ice spells from the flank. Chase heals their gashes and injuries when they get struck by the fire and claws. Eldon throws his spear like a javelin into the dragon's side. It sticks in and he retreats as blood squirts from the dragon's wound. Jonwido casts an ice spell, and a large block of ice appears above the dragon and falls onto it, pinning it to the ground. The dragon turns its long neck around desperately and tries to melt the ice with fire breath but Ramsay rushes in and delivers the death blow to the chest.

It takes three strikes with his sword before the dragon falls to the ground and stops moving.

"Victory!" Ramsay shouts.

Team Leopadillo sit down to catch their breath, exhausted from the battle. They are startled when the dragon begins to speak with a hoarse voice.

"Treacherous men...We will lay waste to your land before our next migration," the dragon says ominously.

"We're going to kill your leader, lizard!" Jonwido answers.

"Why do you call us treacherous?" Ramsay asks.

"In ancient times... your kind has betrayed us... your greed knows no bounds," the dragon says.

"There was a time when dragons and people lived in harmony?" Ramsay asks.

"Yes... but now our king desires only vengeance... on every generation of mankind."

The dragon breathes his last and dies. Ramsay and his comrades return to their horses and drink water to quench their thirst. Peakiboon joins them.

"The dragons don't want to destroy mankind. They

only want to make us suffer every time they return to our land," Chase says.

"As an act of vengeance..." Ramsay adds.

"Then we know they'll be back. We've got to stop them," Eldon says.

"Wow, that was crazy! Fire everywhere!" Peakiboon exclaims.

"Yeah, I'm gonna need new armor soon," Ramsay says as he gestures to the damaged armor.

The ground is burned black at the spot where they fought the dragon. It looks as if a wildfire ravaged the area, except for the glass in the sand.

"The orb! The orb was glowing. Yep!" Peakiboon exclaims.

"Yes, but we need to save it for the alpha dragon," Ramsay says.

"You almost jumped onto the dragon. Just a little higher next time," Chase says to Eldon.

"Damn, it was so close. Practice makes perfect," Eldon says.

The group continues following the railway in the desert. The trees and vegetation of the jungle come into view as they reach the train station at the end of the railway.

The abandoned station is on the edge of the desert and beyond it lies the impenetrable darkness of the jungle.

As their horses step out of the blazing sun onto the shady pathway, Rebel flares his nostrils and stops, clearly uneasy. As Ramsay struggles to urge his reluctant mount further, he wonders if his steed senses more danger ahead.

CHAPTER 5

JUNGLE TRIP

"Finally, we have some shade!" Ramsay exclaims, as they ride through a shady pathway through the trees.

"This is much better," Eldon says.

The chirping of birds and croaking of frogs surrounds them. Ramsay and his team ride until they reach a few native people standing by some huts. The natives call out a greeting to the strangers riding toward them.

"Hello! Come here, warriors! I can see you had a hard journey!" a tribal man says as he waves and smiles.

"Hello! Yes, we come all the way from Ilaburn. A fearsome dragon stood in our way, but we were able to defeat it," Ramsay says.

The clothing worn by Ramsay and his team appears to

have been sprayed with blood. They look like they've come from a war.

"Ah, you are strong warriors indeed. My name is Irkal. This here is Gatthuta, and my son, Llauk. Come and rest with us for a while. We have food and drink. Please. You must be tired," the tribal man says as he opens his arms wide to welcome them.

"They seem friendly enough," Ramsay says quietly to his team.

"I for one could use a rest in this relaxing jungle," Jonwido says.

"Hmm, aren't they a little too friendly? Well, what's the worst that could happen?" Chase says.

"Let's take a break," Ramsay says as he dismounts from his horse.

"Beautiful horse you have. Help yourselves to our horse feed too. That's an interesting pet," Irkal says, as his eyes rest on Peakiboon.

"Hmm, this man is weird," Peakiboon says.

"Come on, don't be rude Peakiboon," Ramsay says firmly.

Our heroes follow Irkal, who is wearing animal skin around his waist and no clothing on his upper body. He brings them to a shaded area with benches made from tree logs. Ramsay and his friends sit down, and Gatthuta serves them a strange fruit that they've never eaten before. It looks like a mango, but the color is purple and blue.

"Here, enjoy the fruit we have. It will refresh and revitalize you," Gatthuta says, as she places two large bowls of fruit on a tree stump.

"Thanks, it looks good. I haven't tried this before," Ramsay says.

"It smells sweet," Chase says.

"Ah this is great," Jonwido says, taking a large bite.

"Yeah, I can eat this all day. Nice," Eldon says.

"I know what you mean. It's sweet but not too sweet," Ramsay says.

Peakiboon goes to one of the bowls to try the fruit. He sniffs a piece and takes a small bite.

"Blah, this stuff is gross. I don't like it. Yuck!" Peakiboon says as he spits it out.

Ramsay and Eldon laugh. Peakiboon wonders how the rest of them could enjoy something so repulsive. *My rabbit taste buds must be more suited to vegetables*, he thinks. Gatthuta also brings the group a couple of jugs filled with juice before disappearing with Irkal for a short while.

"Keep an eye on the big rabbit. It can talk," Irkal whispers to Gatthuta.

Ramsay and his team relax and recount the drama of the day with each other. The sun is setting now, and silhouettes of rocks and trees can be seen against the orange and peach background of the sky. Irkal prepares tents for Ramsay and his teammates to sleep in. More people of the tribe show up, and they begin lighting a bonfire for warmth. It is a mixed society. Many of the people look like they're foreigners. After eating the fruit, the four warriors become calm. They look up at the starry sky and think about home.

THE NEXT DAY, Ramsay and Eldon assist with some work in the village. Jonwido is sleeping late, and Chase is reading a book. Ramsay chops firewood, and Eldon plows soil in the vegetable gardens. Later in the afternoon they come together and sit again by the benches they sat on the day before. They are served more fruit and juice.

"Thank you for helping us with the work around here. Here's some more fruit for your hard work," Gatthuta says.

"Sure, you're welcome. You've treated us well, and the fruit is really good," Ramsay says as he picks up a piece of fruit with a wooden fork.

"I'd like more fruit as well please," Eldon says.

"Me too," Chase says.

"Same here. I can't get enough," Jonwido says.

"Enjoy. Here are some carrots for the rabbit too," Gatthuta says.

After eating the fruit, the team feels relaxed again. All they want to do is just laze around and chat about the good old days. Peakiboon is getting restless though.

"Hey, guys. When are we going to go to the next place? I'm getting kind of bored," Peakiboon asks.

"You want to go already?" Chase asks Peakiboon.

"We have enough time. There's no rush Peakiboon," Ramsay says.

"Yeah, just chill. We need to recharge," Jonwido says.

"Man, a few more days here would be great," Eldon says.

"Yeah, sounds good," Ramsay agrees.

"I want more fruit," Jonwido says.

"You are all so lazy now. I thought you needed to kill the dragons," Peakiboon says.

"It's okay, Peakiboon," Ramsay says.

"Yeah, don't worry. We'll defeat them when we're ready," Chase says.

"Where is all your stuff?" Peakiboon asks.

"They are keeping it safe for us," Ramsay responds and yawns.

"It's in the hut over there," Eldon says.

"Something feels wrong about this," Peakiboon says.

They spend another day at the tribe's village, sitting around the bonfire and chatting with the tribal people at night. It seems like they are getting used to living in this place.

After a few days, Peakiboon realizes that it is the fruit that is making Ramsay and the others behave differently and tries to figure out a way to wake Ramsay up.

How? How can I wake him up? He is always worried about the orb. The precious orb, Yep, Peakiboon thinks to himself. *Where is it?*

Peakiboon sneaks into the hut where they are keeping Ramsay's possessions. His small feet allow him to move very stealthily and quickly. He searches through the bags and finds the dragon shackle orb. He holds it for a while. It is so pretty. After great mental effort, he resists the urge to run away with it and looks for Ramsay. He finds Ramsay sitting in his tent, daydreaming.

"Ramsay! Ramsay! There you are," Peakiboon says.

"Hey Peakiboon," Ramsay responds.

"We must leave. Remember the orb?" Peakiboon says as he holds the orb in front of Ramsay.

"The orb? Wait. Yes, we need to defeat the dragon alpha," Ramsay says.

"Yes. Remember. It's the fruit! Yep. That horrible fruit is making you all lazy. We need to leave," Peakiboon says.

"What? I don't know why we're still in this place. We have a mission to carry out," Ramsay says as he struggles to think rationally.

Ramsay stares at the shackle orb and remembers what happened in Nashia when the dragons attacked. He remembers the advice Galather gave him.

"Dammit! We need to get going," Ramsay exclaims as he forces himself to get up.

"Let's go wake up the others," Peakiboon says.

As Ramsay and Peakiboon leave the tent, Irkal blocks them from passing.

"Oh no you don't," he says.

"Get out of my way," Ramsay says.

"How is this possible? You're supposed to become one of us," Irkal says with a confused expression.

"I see what you're trying to do. We have an important mission. We can't stay here," Ramsay says.

"Guards, restrain him!" Irkal orders.

Two men approach Ramsay to wrestle him and tie him with ropes. Ramsay punches one down, and then kicks at the other one. They fight and Ramsay overpowers them. Ramsay and Peakiboon rush to find the others. Eldon and Chase are lying on blankets on the grass near the eating area.

"What's all the commotion about?" Eldon asks, sleepily.

"We must leave now! Come!" Ramsay shouts.

"What? Why?" Chase asks.

"They are drugging us with the fruits. It's messing with our minds," Ramsay answers.

Peakiboon runs and kicks a bowl of fruit over.

"Okay, let's get the others," Eldon says.

They break into the hut to get their weapons and gear back. Then they search for Jonwido and find him sleeping in a comfortable hammock. They try to wake him up, which is usually a mistake.

"Jonwido, wake up!" Ramsay shouts.

"Seven hells! Get away from me! I'm trying to sleep!" Jonwido shouts angrily.

"We must leave now! The fruits are messing with our heads, man. Irkal was trying to trap us," Eldon shouts.

"What? That whoreson... I can't think straight," Jonwido says.

"We have your staff and gear here. Let's get our horses and go," Ramsay says.

They make their way to the spot where their horses are tied up but are intercepted by several tribesmen wielding weapons. Jonwido tries to cast a spell to electrocute them, but he fails to get the wording right.

"Shit, how do I say the spell again?" Jonwido mumbles as he holds his forehead.

"Never mind, we'll sort them out," Ramsay says.

Ramsay and Eldon take on the tribesmen. Years of fighting terrible monsters have given them impressive reflexes. Even in their stupefied condition, they are too powerful for the tribesmen. Some are knocked out, and the others are killed with the sword and spear.

Ramsay and his team mount their horses and return to the spot where they first met Irkal.

"Which way did we come from again?" Chase asks, trying to recognize the landmarks.

"We need to go that way," Ramsay says, as he points.

"Yes, that looks right," Eldon confirms.

The team continues their journey to the harbor at the gulf of Niparey.

"We should keep going northeast from here to reach The Landing of Rimousby. It's in the fishing village, Bleaklight," Chase says, looking at his compass.

Jonwido is still grumpy at being woken so abruptly. "What did I say about being gullible, Ramsay?" he mutters.

"Well, Ramsay did get us out of there," Eldon says, in Ramsay's defense.

"Peakiboon is the one who got us out. He helped me to snap out of it. You've proven to be a useful ally. Thanks, Peakiboon," Ramsay says.

"Oh? Well done!" Eldon says.

"Aww, thanks!" Peakiboon says.

They ride along the pathway through the jungle, killing a vicious tiger on the way, and arrive at a large wooden archway sign displaying the name, Bleaklight Village. Upon entering the village, the team look for the stables and put their horses away.

"Well, this is it, Rebel. We won't be seeing each other for a while," Ramsay says, stroking his horse.

They ask for directions to the harbor. The wind smells of fish and the salty ocean. Seagulls can be heard mewing and waves crashing in the distance. The walkways along the seaside are made from smooth white rocks. Wooden walkways extend out into the seawater and connect to water platforms where people sit fishing.

Ramsay and his team walk through the village, passing the fish market. They decide to grab a bite to eat on the way. The grilled fish is remarkably tasty to people, but not so much to rabbits. Peakiboon eats some berries they gathered along the way. Huge ships come into view as they reach the harbor. Chase goes to the ticket office to pay the fare for four men and a medium-sized animal to sail to the Port of Somerquet.

"Wow! Big ships!" Peakiboon exclaims.

"Once we land at the Port of Somerquet, it will be a

few days' journey north-west before we reach the city of Shimmerhold," Chase explains to the team.

"What can we expect there?" Eldon asks.

"It's located in the mountains northward. Therefore, I'd expect it to be cold. We should pick up some warm gear when we reach Somerquet," Chase says.

"Our ship departs in about an hour," says Eldon. "We've got some time to kill now."

"Let's look around, but stay away from the stinky fish," Peakiboon says.

"Just make sure you're back here in time," Chase says.

Ramsay excuses himself and finds a quiet place to call Irina. He focuses on the magical linkshard and attempts to connect. The linkshard vibrates and glows.

"Hi," Irina answers.

"Hey, Irina. Did you make it to Bleaklight yet?" Ramsay says.

"Hey, Ramsay. Yeah, we sailed off from there a few days ago. We're at the Port of Somerquet now," Irina says.

"Okay, I'm glad you made it. We had a few... setbacks. We're about to sail from Bleaklight soon," Ramsay replies.

"I hope you don't run into any sea monsters across the ocean. We heard that occasionally they are spotted by ships sailing across," Irina says.

"I was not aware of that. Thanks for the warning," Ramsay says.

"Sorry, I must go now. Bye," Irina says regretfully.

"See ya," Ramsay says, as the linkshard dims.

An hour passes, and everyone boards the ship, ready to depart. The watchkeepers announce the arrival of the ship's captain and ring the bell. A few dozen passengers are on the ship, besides the crew. Some of the passengers are rough, muscular men. A family with kids is on board as well. Some people have brought boxes and other cargo to take with them.

"Have you seen any monsters out in the ocean?" Ramsay asks one of the sailors.

"Aye, we've seen some scary things. Parts of what could belong to a monster have been seen sticking out of the water. I've seen something big myself over the port side, but a sailor who's not willing to sail until all dangers are over will never go out to sea," the sailor says as he helps raise the sails.

"I just want to be prepared," Ramsay says.

"Well, ye look prepared for anything with that armor, lad. Looks like you've been through the mill already," the sailor says.

"Sea monsters? That sounds scary," says Peakiboon timidly. "I've never been on a ship before."

The sailors weigh anchor, and the ship sets sail, gradually reaching cruising speed. It is an overcast day with a moderate breeze. The passengers know that they will be in the open waters for a while. Some are nervous about being at sea while others are in more of a meditative state. Ramsay, Eldon, and Chase are coping well after the first few hours, but not Jonwido. As the ship's motion rises and falls, Jonwido becomes more seasick. He eventually runs to the side of the ship, stands on a box, and blarghh! He throws up everything he ate. His three teammates look on in dismay.

"Oh no," Eldon says.

"Don't you want to give him a heal there, Chase?" Ramsay asks.

"No, let him beg for it," Chase says, as he indifferently looks straight ahead.

"Damn, that's a bit harsh man," Eldon remarks.

"Jonwido is puking! Yuck. So much puke!" Peakiboon exclaims.

There's not much to do on the boat but wait and think. Each of them tries to imagine what the next stretch of the journey is going to entail when they land. This is also a time for them to consider the situation they're in. The comforts of home are nowhere near. There is no turning back now. Chase thinks of his lover back home.

He has never been out on a mission this long. He wonders if he'll see her again.

Ramsay has a laser focus on the task at hand. How would he use the orb at the right moment? He memorizes the written incantation. Eldon listens to the sounds of the ship on the water while doing squats. Jonwido is in a dark space. He is obviously still grieving the loss of his family back home. The team just allows him to be. He is a black mage after all. Perhaps the pain would fuel his destructive abilities.

Suddenly the ship shudders and tilts upwards as if something has collided with it. Everyone trips and falls from the shaking movement.

"What was that?" someone shouts.

"Did we hit something?" another person shouts.

Something huge and smooth bobs up to the surface of the water and then sinks gain. Then a massive tentacle, with big suction cups under it, comes straight out of the sea on the starboard side and smashes down onto the deck. People scream in terror.

"Mayday! Mayday! Mayday! We're under attack!" the sailors cry out.

"Triton's balls! A sea monster?" the captain shouts, stepping out of the bridge to see what's going on.

Dammit Irina, you jinxed it! Ramsay thinks.

Ramsay and his team gather and draw their weapons

to defend themselves. More tentacles rear up out of the water and knock people around. Barrels are thrown around the deck and wooden floorboards are broken. Peakiboon scurries about, looking for a place to hide.

"What is that? A giant octopus?" Eldon shouts, above the terrified screaming of the passengers.

"Yes, or something related to one. It's massive!" Chase says.

A tentacle moves towards Ramsay, but he cuts it off with a powerful slice before it can slam him. A low bellow echoes from the water as the beast roars in pain. A tentacle slithers along the wooden deck and grabs one of the boxes. A load of cheese falls out as it breaks open. The other tentacles also grab boxes of cheese and pull them down into the water.

"It's after the cheese!" Chase shouts.

"Someone just had to bring their whole collection of cheese with them on the ship," Ramsay complains.

"Unfortunately, it's also grabbing people," Eldon points out.

"People and cheese... must be this octopus's favorite snack," Jonwido says.

It is chaos on board the vessel as people try to escape the long arms of the octopus. Peakiboon looks behind him and sees a tentacle coming after him. He screams and runs from it. It follows closely behind him. Backed into a corner, he covers his eyes with his paws expecting the tentacle to grab him, but it quickly changes direction and grabs a box.

One of the tentacles hits Jonwido into the air. He rolls on the deck as he lands. In retaliation, he casts an ice spell and shoots the tentacle with a freezing mist. It freezes solid and then breaks into small pieces of ice. He does the same attack on another tentacle, and it also breaks off into pieces. The monster octopus bellows again, and the remaining tentacles retract back into the ocean. It has lost three limbs now and has apparently decided to retreat. The passengers slowly settle down and attend to their injuries.

The crew throws the remaining boxes of cheese overboard at Chase's instruction.

Jonwido has been the most affected in the battle. He feels tired and weak and falls to his knees. Chase takes pity on him and casts a healing spell to restore his vitality, and an aura of light appears around him.

"Many thanks, warriors. We're in your debt. Help yourselves to our ship's rum," the captain says.

"Yeah, let's have some rum," Eldon says.

"I don't mind if I do," Jonwido says. It's obvious he's already feeling better.

"Nice job freezing the tentacles," Ramsay says.

The sailors and those standing on the deck give a loud cheer for Ramsay's team. The giant tentacle that Ramsay chopped off is lying on the floor nearby. It is a lot of meat to waste, considering that it is longer and thicker than a shark with suction cups the size of dinner plates. They decide to give it to the chief cook to prepare for the passengers to feast on.

"These people will eat anything. Yep," Peakiboon says as he pokes the tentacle.

CHAPTER 6

GIANT PROBLEMS

The members of Team Pandeaqead unwind outside a tavern in Somerquet as they engage in idle talk.

"What's the plan again?" Verdan asks, as he leans against a wall with his arms crossed.

"The next stop is Shimmerhold, and then we wait for Ramsay's team," Irina says.

"Why do we need to wait for them?" Romulus asks.

"They have a dragon shackle orb. Do you have a better idea of how we're going to beat the dragon alpha?" Irina asks.

"Uhm..." Romulus hesitates as he furrows his brow.

"Yeah, I didn't think so," Irina interrupts him.

"And we must help *Ramsay,* right?" Phinara smiles and giggles as she teases Irina.

Irina tries to keep a poker face but a playful smile flits across her face as she turns to Phinara.

"We could kill the alpha if I use my deadly ninjutsu arts," Verdan says, trying to look cool.

"Hah yeah, like that other time with the gorilla boss?" Irina says, making fun of Verdan's tendency to choke in monster fights.

"Hey! That was just bad luck! That banana peel came out of nowhere," Verdan says nervously as he straightens himself.

"All I need is my axe to kill a monster, but a dragon? That's a different story," Romulus says.

Verdan is skilled in the lethal ways of the ninja. His moves are impressive to behold. However, his self-conscious and vain personality causes him to become distracted sometimes. Romulus has incredible physical power and can split boulders with his huge axe, but he is not the brightest one around. The monsters that they encounter on missions are usually more amused at their antics than intimidated. Irina is an archer. She's the one who keeps the team in order and finishes off the enemy with her arrows. Phinara does an amazing job keeping the team alive with her healing and protective skills.

"Where do you think the dragon orb comes from?" Romulus asks.

"I have no idea, but apparently it can take out any

dragon and grant wishes, buddy! We'll have to ask Ramsay how he got his hands on one," Verdan responds expressively.

A stranger in the bar overhears the chatter going on outside and moves closer to the team.

Dragon orb, huh? he thinks as he listens inconspicuously to Verdan and Romulus.

IRINA and her team are sufficiently rested and prepare for their journey to Shimmerhold. They get their horses and ride out into the cold wilderness, passing the ruin of the church of Logrushi on the way. The landscape changes from green and hilly to craggy and mountainous as they get closer to the city of Shimmerhold.

The sky darkens, and they find a spot to camp for the night.

At sunrise, they continue their journey. The temperature drops rapidly, and the ground becomes snowy. Their horses leave deep hoof prints in the snow as they pick their way cautiously towards the snow-capped mountain range in the distance. Fortunately, they came prepared with cold-insulating fur clothes to keep them warm.

As they approach a mountain pass, a loud growl reverberates around them. It is like the sound of a troll but much louder. The ground rumbles as a giant jumps down the side of the mountain and lands a short distance in front of Irina and her team. The giant is wearing light armor covering most of its torso. It also has a colossal sword in its right hand. Its skin is a teal blue color, and monstrous canines protrude from its bottom jaw.

"It's a snow giant!" Verdan shouts.

"Oh boy, this is not good," Irina says.

"What do we do?" Romulus asks.

"We stand our ground," Irina says as the giant lumbers slowly toward them.

"Look out for its sword and aim for the legs!" Phinara shouts.

Romulus dismounts from his horse and runs ahead to keep the attention off the others. The giant stops and pulls its arm back to prepare for a horizontal sword sweep. Its movements are slow and easy to read, but it would be better to dodge than to block, considering the massive size of its sword. Romulus reads the attack and retreats out of reach of the sword which creates a deep circular cut in the snow as it ploughs the ground like a child drawing a line in the sand with a stick. Verdan vanishes and reappears near the giant's shoulder and throws a smoke bomb at its head. A cloud of smoke surrounds the giant's head as Verdan draws his knives and launches himself at the giant's head.

The giant roars as it swings its arms wildly, and Verdan

tumbles down into the snow. Irina and Phinara remain on their horses, who are snorting and backing away in fear. Romulus bolts at the towering giant again and tries to attack its leg with his axe. Clang! It blocks with the sword and hits Romulus away, causing him to fall on his back. Verdan maneuvers around and throws several shuriken stars into the giant's back. The projecting blades are ineffective against its hard skin. The giant turns around to kick Verdan, but he swiftly dodges. A couple of Irina's arrows strike the giant's torso but do not penetrate deep enough. Romulus and Verdan fall back.

"Our attacks are not working!" Irina shouts desperately.

"It's got thick skin and durable armor," Verdan points out.

"That huge-ass sword is a problem too," Romulus says.

"It's coming for another attack!" Phinara shouts.

Irina quickly fires two arrows at the giant's head. It covers its face and receives the arrows in its left forearm while it moves toward them. Phinara casts a barrier spell, and a large wall of light forms to shield them. The giant pounds the wall with his fists and hits it with the sword. The barrier takes damage with each hit but holds up.

"This shield is not going to last long," Phinara says.

"We need to retreat," Irina says.

"Yes, this guy's just too much," Verdan agrees.

Irina's team mount their horses and flee from the giant. Behind them, they can hear him breaking through the shield but by the time he gets through they are out of sight. Once safe, they discuss their options and agree to return to Somerquet and ask Ramsay's team to assist with fighting the giant mountain guardian.

MEANWHILE, Ramsay's ship arrives at the Somerquet harbor. The ship drifts close to the pier before being towed with smaller boats to the mooring using long, heavy ropes.

"We made it! We made it! Yep," Peakiboon exclaims.

"Finally, we're here," Ramsay says.

"Land, at last," Jonwido says as he quickly walks over the gangway with excitement.

"Next time you board for free, warriors," the captain says. "The monster insurance would be enough fare."

The rest of the team disembark onto the pier, and explore the harbor, searching for a tavern. They follow the wooden walkway and come across a stall selling interesting items.

"Hold on, they have unusual potions here," Chase says. "Do you have any potions for curing frost?"

"Yes, look over here," the merchant replies.

"Ah, those are colorful bottles," Peakiboon says longingly.

"I need to get some healing potions as well," Ramsay says.

Our warriors purchase some potions and then continue their way.

"We need to pick up warm gear as well, preferably fur coats," Chase advises.

"I can feel the cold already," Jonwido says.

"Let's take a break at a tavern first. I haven't had a good meal in a while," Eldon says.

"This tastes good," Peakiboon says as he drinks a potion.

"Wait, did you pay for that, Peakiboon?" Ramsay asks.

"Pay? With what money?" Peakiboon asks.

"Never mind," Ramsay says with a long sigh, placing a coin in the merchant's waiting hand.

After walking a while, and passing many strangers, the group follows the sound of music to the door of a tavern. There are a variety of races and cultures here. Dwarves, elves, kobolds, and humans walk by. Written on the front, above the entrance, are the words "The Oceanic Ferret". Ramsay and his team enter the tavern and find a table. They order food and drinks and relax as they enjoy casual conversation.

"I'm glad they serve roast chicken here," Jonwido says.

"Yeah, for sure," Eldon agrees.

"Hey Ramsay, still got the orb?" Chase asks.

"Yeah, I've got it," Ramsay replies.

"I love looking at the orb! Yep. It's so pretty!" Peakiboon says expressively.

After a while, a tall stranger with long red hair walks up to Ramsay. He's wearing silver armor and carries a huge, black, two-handed greatsword on his back. A long, flowing, black cape hangs down behind him.

"Oi, are you Ramsay?" the stranger asks.

"Yes, that's my name," Ramsay says as he turns to look at the person speaking.

"Have you always had bad luck, or have you been saving it all up for today?" the stranger asks, tauntingly.

"What do you mean?" Ramsay says as his expression becomes serious.

Ramsay's team all stares at the stranger.

"My name is Garth. You have something I want – the dragon orb. You don't look like the kind of man who'd just hand it over peacefully. I challenge you to a duel. Whoever wins, gets the orb," Garth says as the group becomes dead silent.

Jonwido grunts as he reaches for his staff.

"You're going to have to go—" Eldon says before being interrupted by Ramsay.

"It's fine. I got this," Ramsay says to his team, rising slowly to his feet.

"That's what I like to hear!" Garth says as he flashes a manic grin at Ramsay.

The two warriors walk outside, and Ramsay hands the bag with the dragon orb to Chase. He faces Garth, sizing him up as they stand a short distance apart. Spectators start to gather around as the people realize what's happening. Ramsay stretches a little and firmly grips his longsword and shield. Garth draws his greatsword, and it grates metal-lically as he drops the point onto the stony ground. The duel commences and they move toward each other in their battle stances.

"Even if Ramsay loses, I'm not letting that asshole take the orb," Jonwido says softly.

"I'm with you man. There's a lot at stake," Eldon says nodding.

Garth strikes first, swinging his sword diagonally. His attacks have a great deal of power behind them. Ramsay lifts his shield and blocks the attack, countering with a forward sword thrust. Garth dodges and moves to the side. Ramsay moves closer and strikes with a combination of horizontal and diagonal swings, but Garth parries them and kicks Ramsay away. Garth attacks with a straight swing from top to bottom and Ramsay dodges to the side as the greatsword strikes the ground. Ramsay lands a hit and cuts Garth's armor with an upward diagonal slash.

Garth leaps backward and raises the greatsword above his head. He slashes the greatsword downwards, sending an energy wave out of the tip of his blade. The wave flies at Ramsay, damaging him before he could block. The spectators standing behind Ramsay try to jump out of the way. Garth attacks a few more times in the same way, throwing energy waves at Ramsay with slashes. This time Ramsay dodges and blocks them.

"Okay, let's use magic," Ramsay says.

Ramsay raises his sword and points it at the ground where Garth is standing. He casts a spell, and a huge energetic sword of light comes straight out of the ground, flashing about Garth as he tries to get out of the way. The fight continues for a while, each of them launching and parrying strikes like seasoned swordsmen.

Eventually, Ramsay gains the upper hand. He parries an attack from the greatsword and swiftly knocks Garth off his feet. As Garth lands on his back with a crash, the tip of Ramsay's sword stops at his neck.

Ramsay is the clear winner, but as he turns to walk away, Garth gets up and charges at Ramsay in a fit of rage.

"This is a duel!" Garth shouts as he attempts to swing the greatsword at Ramsay.

Ramsay quickly extends his sword and spins around

with a counterattack. Blood splatters on the ground as Garth's left hand is sliced clean off. The spectators gasp at the violence. Garth curses and roars in agony and Ramsay and the team leave the scene, as a bystander rushes to wrap a piece of his cape around the stump to reduce the bleeding.

Ramsay and his team rest at an inn for the evening and in the morning, they meet up at the marketplace to buy warmer clothes and weapons.

"My armor has served me well. It's about time for an upgrade. This should keep me warm in the snow," Ramsay says.

"These pieces look like they're made from wolf skins. They're quite comfortable," Eldon says.

Ramsay eventually buys clothes with metal framing inside for heavy protection. The rest of the team takes lighter clothing. Each of them contributes some money to purchase Peakiboon a small jacket.

"Ah! This fits snugly! Yep," Peakiboon says.

"Hey! Ramsay!" a familiar voice calls.

Ramsay turns to look where the voice is coming from and sees Irina and her team approach.

"Hi! Good to see you," Ramsay greets them warmly.

"We're lucky to find you here," Irina says.

"Your girlfriend is here, Ramsay!" Peakiboon shouts.

"Haha, don't mind the rabbit," Ramsay says with a

weak smile.

"Quiet, Peakiboon," Ramsay hisses through his teeth.

"Aww, what a cute jacket he's wearing," Irina says, giggling at Peakiboon.

"Shouldn't you be further ahead by now?" Ramsay asks.

"We were stopped by a snow giant and had to come back," Romulus says, emphasizing the size of the giant with his deep voice.

"A snow giant? Eldon questions.

"Yeah, it was guarding the mountain pass on the way to Shimmerhold," Irina answers.

"I see. I thought we may have to deal with a mountain guardian," Chase says as he touches his chin.

"I was hoping your team could join us to defeat the snow giant together," Irina says.

"Yeah, not a problem. We were planning on taking that route anyway," Ramsay says eagerly.

"Isn't there another route to Shimmerhold? One without giants?" Eldon asks.

"Yes, but the weather would make it difficult to navigate and ride horses. One cannot assume that it would be safe either," Chase responds.

"Right..." Eldon says.

"Looks like we're all traveling together then," Phinara says.

"That's right, sweet cheeks!" Jonwido says as he gives a wolf whistle.

"Uf! Don't call me that, dwarf," Phinara responds, irritated and angry.

"She didn't like that, man," Eldon warns Jonwido with a nervous tone.

"That lady is scary," Peakiboon says, putting his ears in front of his face.

The group goes to the stables to get horses before leaving. The horses in this part of the country are shaggy and more suitable for cold weather. Rays of sunshine break through the overcast sky as Ramsay and the group of warriors set out to the city of Shimmerhold.

Eventually, they reach the mountains and draw near the pass where Irina's team fought the giant. They leave their horses in a safe spot, and proceed on foot, searching for the enemy.

"It's probably around here somewhere. It jumped off the ledge up there, last time," Irina points out.

"The giant is enormous. Prepare yourselves," Verdan says to the group.

"I'll tank it while you chop it down like a tree. Right Romulus?" Ramsay asks.

"That sounds good to me," Romulus agrees.

Nearby trees begin to rustle and shake as the snow falls off them. The giant slowly emerges and sees the group of people. It gives a roar and lifts up its sword.

"Here he is. Let's go!" Ramsay says, as he steps purposefully forward towards the giant.

The giant attacks Ramsay with its sword as the rest of the team gets into position. The blows from its sword are awfully heavy, and Ramsay executes a spell to increase his physical defense. Peakiboon screams and hops behind Irina.

"I got you," Chase says as he focuses on healing Ramsay.

Eldon sprints to the flank of the giant and leaps high into the air. He stabs his spear into the giant's right bicep and jumps off again. As the giant's head swivels slowly towards Eldon, Romulus runs toward the legs. Verdan, feeling a bit like a third wheel, executes Kuji Kiri hand signs and creates several clones of himself that dash in and distract the giant. Romulus sees an opportunity and strikes the left leg multiple times with his axe.

The giant roars and falls to his knees, confused by being attacked from many directions. It raises both of its arms above its head and slams them down, creating a shockwave around it. Ramsay, Romulus, and Eldon are knocked to the ground. Verdan's clones disappear into smoke. Jonwido takes the opportunity to deal some damage and casts a spell to launch a couple of large fireballs at the giant which explode against its chest.

The giant is momentarily dazed by the explosions but returns its attention to the warriors nearby. It sweeps the sword in the direction of Ramsay and Romulus, hitting them off their feet. Chase and Phinara are busy healing wounds and injuries as fast as they can. Eldon jumps again and stabs his spear into an open spot near the back of the giant's neck. Jonwido shoots a few more fireballs as the giant holds its arms up to block them.

Irina draws her bow and fires several large electric arrows at the giant. They strike the giant's face and torso like lightning bolts. With a roar of pain, the giant topples slowly forward, and the earth vibrates as it hits the ground with a bone-jarring crash. Ramsay runs over and plunges his sword into its neck to finish it off.

The snow giant has been defeated.

The party cheers over their cooperative victory. They slowly walk back to their horses, catching their breath.

"Hey, how'd you learn to jump like that?" Verdan asks Eldon while he walks with him.

"Oh, I've been practicing so that I'll be able to strike dragons mid-air. I need to jump higher though," Eldon replies.

"That's pretty cool," Verdan says.

"Thanks. It was cool when you made copies of yourself too," Eldon reciprocates.

"Oh yeah that's one of my shinobi skills," Verdan says with a grin.

"You had great timing with those shots," Ramsay says to Irina.

"Thanks, I couldn't have done it without you," Irina responds.

The group of warriors make their way up the mountain pass. They find another dead snow giant lying on the side of the path, with pools of blood staining the snow.

"It looks like there was an epic battle here," Ramsay says.

"Yes, it could be that one of the other teams made it here before us," Chase says.

After following the path for a while, they arrive at a frozen lake, which extends as far as the eye can see in every direction. The group deliberates whether it's safe to cross over. Bang! Jonwido hurls large rocks onto the ice with his gravity magic. The rocks make chips in the ice, but it remains solid.

"Well, that's one way to test it," Eldon says.

"Looks like it's safe," Irina says.

"I've got big rocks!" Jonwido says and winks at Phinara.

"Ugh, who would've guessed," Phinara says as she

looks away.

Verdan and Romulus laugh.

They ride slowly over the frozen lake. It is difficult to move as their horses' hooves slip on the ice. Chase falls off his horse as it slides. Verdan's horse tumbles as well, throwing him down. The rest of them dismount. Apparently, this was not a good idea. The teams lead the horses carefully and make it across the frozen lake together.

As they journey further, the city walls of Shimmerhold come into view. They approach the stairway and ride up to the huge gate.

"From what I've read about Shimmerhold, they have strange laws. Be careful about what you do and speak. Especially you, Jon," Chase says as he instructs the group.

"Meh," Jonwido says with a shrug.

Two sentries stand at the gate, wearing impressive armor and holding spears. They stop the group and ask them what business they have in Shimmerhold. Ramsay tells the truth and explains that they're just passing through and would only be there a few days at most. The sentry checks their bags and supplies.

"The creature has no diseases, does it?" the sentry asks concerning Peakiboon.

"No, he's just our pet. He's quite docile," Ramsay answers.

"All right if he doesn't shit where he's not supposed to.

Seeing as you're willing to brave giants to get here, you may all pass," the sentry says.

The gates are opened, and the teams enter the city. Shortly after riding in, they pass the gallows.

"They definitely want everyone to see what happens to criminals here," Ramsay says.

"Yeah, no kidding," Eldon says.

"Many receive the death sentence for, what we would consider, minor offences," Chase explains.

They continue, admiring the architecture. The buildings are elaborate and beautiful statues decorate the public areas. Snow lies in the pristine streets. The teams' horses are deposited at the stables.

A group of priests can be seen walking a short distance away, wearing tall miters on their heads, apparently on their way to the grand church up ahead. The citizens don't seem very friendly and glance suspiciously at the visitors. A pipe organ can be heard playing in the distance.

"I'm going to search for the mages' guild. Let's convene here tomorrow," Chase says.

"I'm coming with you," Ramsay says.

"Cool, I'm going to explore a bit. Maybe find something to eat," Eldon says.

"Okay, we'll see you later," Irina says.

The group splits up. Irina, Phinara, and Peakiboon go off in one direction. Eldon, Verdan, Jonwido, and

Romulus walk away in another direction. Ramsay and Chase go on to ask around for the mages' guild.

"Are we going to ask for directions to Yragos?" Ramsay asks as his metal sabatons clack on the cobblestones.

"I already know the way to Yragos. What I want to find out is if they know where the Alpha's lair is, and how to get there."

"Okay, good idea."

"The scholars of the Shimmerhold mages' guild are famous in Aegemald," Chase says.

Ramsay and Chase ask officials whom they find standing around for directions. After walking through the city for a while, going up stairs, passing through alleyways, and making a few turns they reach the door to the guild. A crest is on the door with the words "As above, so below" written under it. They enter a large, circular room. Books are placed on shelves all around the walls. It looks like an extensive library, and numerous people are walking around and sitting inside.

The people are wearing robes and hats of various styles and colors. Ramsay and his friend walk up to the reception.

"Ah, you must be warriors from Nashia," the receptionist says, drily.

"Well, yes. How did you know?" Ramsay responds.

"We've had a few others like you come in here recently.

You want to know about the dragon's lair, is that correct?"

"Yes," Ramsay and Chase answer together.

"Wait here. I will find out if the High Magus is available now," the receptionist says as she turns and walks down the hall.

They wait a few minutes, and the receptionist returns.

"You may go through. It's down the hall, to the right, and the third door on your right,"

"Thank you," Chase says.

Ramsay and Chase enter the High Magus's office.

"Welcome, warriors," the magus says with a slight smile. "My name is Izadius."

"Greetings, sir," Chase says.

"Good day, sir," Ramsay says, formally.

"I take it the two of you want to know where the alpha dragon's lair is. Other warriors from Nashia came in a few days ago looking for the same information. We are aware of the fact that the dragons have returned from their hidden world. The warriors mentioned that they are on a mission to kill the alpha. I thought it was foolishness, but they remained serious about it. So, I told them what I know. How do you plan on defeating the alpha?" Izadius asks.

"We possess a dragon shackle orb. My master, Galather, gave it to me in Nashia. We will use it to slay the alpha," Ramsay explains.

"Aah, Elder Galather entrusted you with one of the

remaining dragon orbs? This changes things. You have a real chance of completing your mission. Where is the rest of your team?"

"We are eight in total. The other six are walking about the city," Chase says.

"You have a better chance with such a large team. All right, I will tell you how you could reach the dragon's lair. The alpha dragon resides in the largest mountain in the floating islands of Eivulth. To get there you must travel to the temple of Acohr, make it to the end of the inner chamber, and use the ancient teleporter there. Using the teleporter should be easy, but it's guarded by a monster. The teleporter will take you directly to Eivulth. From there you would be able to reach the lair on foot. Keep in mind that Eivulth is probably swarming with dragons. It would be best if you sneak inside the lair undetected," Izadius explains gravely.

"Oh, that makes sense. Thank you for the information," Chase says.

"Thank you. This allows us to devise a plan for the next part of our journey. I'll inform the others," Ramsay adds.

"I hope you succeed in your mission. We are safe from the dragons here in Shimmerhold because of the cold, but the rest of the realm is in great danger. May the gods be with you."

Chapter 7

The Legend of Ice

Izadius sits in his office, reading up on the history of Eivulth.

4320 years ago, in a city in Yragos called Qreim, a ruler discusses his treacherous plans with the members of his court.

"Are the alchemists done with creating all the dragon shackle orbs?" Emperor Andryr asks.

"Yes, my Lord. All the orbs are ready, and the teleporter is functional. We may proceed to Eivulth," Chief Sage Uphiar says.

Andryr strokes his thick beard as he sits comfortably on the throne. His long, blond hair is held in place with the glittering crown.

"All is going according to plan. Soon I will have a good deal of wishes at my disposal. The dragons are too trusting.

They will not see it coming," Emperor Andryr says, laughing sadistically.

"The greater the wish, the greater the amount of energy required of the orb. If you desire immortality, my Lord, we will need the energy of the alpha," Uphiar says.

"See that it's done. Do not fail me," Emperor Andryr says.

A company of knights, mages, generals, and soldiers waits by the teleporter as the engineers prepare to activate it. Everyone is given a dragon shackle orb and given instructions on how to use it.

"In the dragon kingdom, no one is to attack without an order. Be friendly until told otherwise," the chief sage commands.

The company confirms that they understand. The teleporter is turned on, and they all disappear as they march into it. In Eivulth, everyone marches out of the teleporter located there and waits for further orders. The local dragons welcome the men, having expected their arrival.

Uphiar tells the dragons that he's the emissary from Qreim, and requests to meet their leader. The dragons lead them to a meeting place on a plateau and let them know that their king will be with them shortly. Uphiar then tells the generals to instruct the men to wait for his signal. Soon the alpha is seen flying with several powerful dragons to the plateau. Many smaller dragons are also accompanying him. His long, majestic form descends in front of the men, and he starts speaking in a thunderous voice.

"Ah, men of Yragos, welcome. We have been expecting you."

"It is an honor to stand before you in this beautiful kingdom, your Highness. We have something to show you," Uphiar says as he gives the signal to his men.

Uphiar's company moves forward, taking out their shackle orbs and holding them out at arm's length. They recite the incantations, and each orb starts pulling energy out of a dragon nearby. Streaks of different colored energy move around in the air. The dragons are startled and roar, not knowing what is going on. The smaller dragons collapse to the ground first. The shackle orbs shine brightly in the hands of the hardened men.

"What is the meaning of this?" the alpha cries out in horror.

Uphiar's orb locks onto the alpha, absorbing its energy. The dragon struggles and flies upwards, breaking free of the orb tether. In the air, the alpha charges up and releases a massive blast of fire and light at Andryr's army, killing a fraction of them.

"It's too powerful. Retreat! Retreat!" Uphiar commands.

A couple of the elite dragons are drained. Uphiar's company races to return to the teleporter, having powered up more than a dozen orbs. The alpha is furious at the betrayal. The lesser dragons flee in fear, but he pursues the men, picking them off one by one. Uphiar tries to bind the alpha with a spell, but he's too fast in the sky. He resorts to impeding it by putting up a large barrier of magic. Uphiar and the rest of the company reach the teleporter and escape the dragon's wrath, but they manage to bring several orbs containing dragon energy back with them.

"I shall have my revenge on mankind!" the alpha shouts as he breathes fire.

AN HOUR LATER, Uphiar walks into the throne room with several men carrying a chest where Emperor Andryr sits on his throne in the palace in Qreim. They approach the throne and place the chest down. The sound of it touching the floor echoes around the spacious, quiet room.

"Please tell me you have good news, chief sage," Emperor Andryr says.

"We returned with six orbs, my Lord. Unfortunately, we could not capture the alpha's energy, and had to escape," Uphiar says, avoiding the emperor's gaze.

"What? That is the one thing I specifically wanted! What use are these feeble orbs?"

"They're still very useful, your majesty. You could wish for wealth, power, and other wonderful things."

"But not immortality!" the emperor shouts furiously, spittle flying from his mouth.

An adviser rushes into the room and tells the emperor that there is an emergency. Dragons have been spotted in the city and are causing destruction.

"What are dragons weak against?" Emperor Andryr asks.

"Ice, sir," Uphiar answers.

Andryr opens a chest and grabs one of the dragon orbs. He wishes to have the ability to cast the most powerful ice spells. The orb flashes and grants him his wish.

"If it's a war they want, it's a war they'll get," Andryr says, as he laughs maniacally.

The emperor goes out into the city and joins the soldiers in the battle. The terrifying form of the alpha dragon glides over the city, and many others surround him. A large dragon swoops down near Andryr. He raises his hand at it, and a blizzard surrounds the dragon, freezing it immediately. More dragons fly down and try to attack him, but he freezes all of them with blizzard attacks. The alpha realizes what is happening and calls his warriors back.

"You may win this battle, but two thousand years from

now you will be gone, and I will return," the alpha dragon exclaims.

Emperor Andryr attempts to attack the alpha and his dragons with a gigantic snowstorm, but they flee into the sky.

This is the legend of the Ice Emperor Andryr.

CHAPTER 8

THE ORB ORDEAL

Armed with new knowledge, Ramsay proceeds to meet his comrades gathered at the meeting place in Shimmerhold. He informs the group of what the high magus said and explains that their next destination is the temple of Acohr in Yragos. They decide to rest another day in Shimmerhold before going out into the snow again. The following day the group meets near the western city gate, prepared for the journey. Their horses are packed with food and supplies. They wait patiently for everyone to show up.

"Did you go to any taverns?" Ramsay asks Eldon.

"It was weird. We found no taverns. There are some places that serve warm meals, but no alcohol," Eldon replies.

"Oh, that must have been disappointing for Jon."

"Yeah," Eldon says as he chuckles.

"I'm keen to leave this freezing land," Jonwido says.

Verdan and Romulus arrive.

"The next stop is the town of Kine. Once we've rested, we'll journey from there to the temple," Chase says.

Leaving Shimmerhold behind, they ride through the snow. The path westward winds downhill for a while before turning left into a rocky valley. They trot along for two hours until there is no snow or ice under their hooves. The environment becomes particularly green with multiple small rivers crossing it. The sunlight sparkles in the water streams. The ground is covered with lush grass, and there are glades of tall trees. It is time for the warriors to stop and rest the horses for a while.

Everyone dismounts and removes their winter clothing gratefully.

"Ah, what a change," Jonwido says, removing his furry headgear.

They relax beneath the trees, enjoying the warm weather. Ramsay and his team sit on the side of a grassy slope in the shade. Peakiboon enjoys the attention and cuddles he receives from the girls.

"Aww, come here, Peakiboon," Phinara calls.

Peakiboon hops over and she starts petting him. She holds Peakiboon close to her. He smiles as he looks at her breast and leans against it.

"Hmm, I think that rabbit is enjoying himself a bit too much," Verdan says, squinting at Peakiboon.

"Aww, he's just a big baby bunny," Irina says.

"It's more like a big naughty bunny," Romulus says with a blank expression.

Verdan shakes his head.

"So, this is Yragos. It's kind of nice. It makes me feel like building a log cabin," Eldon says.

Jonwido stares in Eldon's direction and his eyes widen.

"There's something behind you," Jonwido says, pointing behind Eldon's shoulder.

Eldon turns around and comes face to face with an elemental being.

"Oh, it's a sylph," Eldon says as he laughs.

"Hey little guy," Ramsay says.

The sylph is small and has youthful features like a child. Its eyes are black, and its frilly wings resemble those of a butterfly. It is wearing clothing made from tiny leaves, which have been delicately stitched together. A visible aura spirals around the sylph with a light green hue. It giggles as it bounces around slowly. Two more of them show up. They are friendly and pleasant to watch.

"Wow, they're beautiful," Irina says.

"Hi there," Phinara says as a sylph passes by.

The warriors enjoy their lunch and the break while their horses graze and drink from the clear stream. They're all tempted to linger for a few more hours, and no one makes a move, but Ramsay knows he must motivate the others.

"We need to get going again," he says.

"Yes, let's get to Kine before dark. This is unfamiliar territory. We don't know what could be lurking about," Chase says as he stands up.

They say goodbye to the sylphs and continue on their way.

Eventually, our heroes reach the town of Kine. Most of the houses and structures are made from wood. There are many farm animals roaming around, and some are kept in pens. The locals seem to be more down-to-earth compared to the citizens of the previous cities. It is sunset, and the group splits up. Ramsay and Irina walk off together looking for a place to sleep for the night. Fighting together has deepened their connection.

"It's been a while since we've had time alone. I've missed you," Ramsay says.

"I've missed you too. It's crazy. I haven't felt this comfortable with someone so quickly before," Irina responds.

"Yeah, it's like I've known you for months," Ramsay says.

"Nothing builds trust more than facing death together," Irina says.

"...and coming out victorious. We're almost at the final stretch," Ramsay says.

"How do you feel about that?" Irina asks.

"Anticipation, dread, excitement, revenge... I have many feelings at the moment."

"We're gonna do it. Don't worry."

THE NEXT MORNING, Ramsay meets up with his team members and they proceed to the stables to wait for Irina and the others.

"We have to say goodbye here, buddy," Ramsay says to Peakiboon.

"The next part of our journey is going to be too dangerous for you," Chase adds.

"I'm going to miss you guys. Yep," Peakiboon says as his eyes become teary.

"We'll see you again on our way back. First, we have a really big dragon to slay," Ramsay says.

"Congrats, Rabbit, we didn't eat you," Jonwido says.

They give Peakiboon a few coins to buy food, and he

shuffles sadly towards a field of grazing sheep. Irina arrives with her friends, and they look worriedly at the drooping figure of the departing rabbit.

"I hope Peakiboon will be all right," Irina says.

"I hope *we'll* be all right," Verdan says with a nervous grin.

With the tingle of adrenaline in their veins, they set out in the direction of the temple of Acohr.

On the way, the teams ride past an area with patches of scorched grass and charred trees. It's an ominously familiar scene.

"Be alert! A dragon may be nearby," Ramsay shouts.

Each one is silent, but vigilant, as they trot along. Suddenly, a red dragon appears, gliding over the trees. It tilts its head and roars as it spots the group. Everyone climbs off their horses and takes cover.

"I've been preparing for this!" Eldon shouts.

The dragon banks and flies toward the warriors. Phinara prepares to get a shield up. Ramsay unsheathes his sword, but Eldon runs past him, leaps above the dragon's head and drops down, plunging his spear into its neck. Then he jumps off with a backflip, and lands on his feet, holding his spear triumphantly above his head while blood gushes from the dragon's neck. It falls to the ground, sliding and breaking trees until it stops. The dragon chokes and bleeds momentarily and then dies.

Everyone in the group stands wide-eyed, gaping at the dead dragon.

"Eldon, you just killed a dragon with one hit," Ramsay says, stunned.

"I did. Yes! I did," Eldon says as he laughs.

"Wow!" Verdan says.

"Incredible," Chase says.

"That was amazing," Irina says.

"Nice, keep it up," Jonwido says.

"Now I know why Galather had that message for you," Ramsay says.

They applaud and cheer for Eldon's accomplishment. Ramsay walks over to the dragon's corpse and cuts off a small piece of one of its horns. He hands it to Eldon as a souvenir, who puts it proudly into his saddlebag.

***

THE TEAMS GET BACK on the path to the temple and ride for another three hours. Upon arriving at the location, they identify the entrance to a massive stone temple carved into the mountain rock. They dismount from their horses and leave them loosely tied to overhanging branches near a juicy patch of grass.

"This is it. We need to tread carefully as there are likely to be many ancient booby traps inside," Chase says.

"Fortunately, traps are my specialty," Verdan says, holding out his hands in a welcoming gesture.

"Okay, lead the way then," Irina says impatiently.

"Umm sure, follow me," Verdan says as he walks in front.

They enter the temple.

"It's dark," Verdan complains, as he struggles to adjust to the dim light.

Chase and Phinara cast spells and small balls of light appear on the top of their heads, acting as torches, allowing them to see inside.

"Thanks," Verdan says, almost hoping that they couldn't proceed.

They walk through a stone passageway. There are ancient, undecipherable symbols painted on the walls. Faint sounds of flapping of wings echo from the high ceiling. The temple is filled with a musty odor.

"Stop!" Verdan says urgently, scanning the floor ahead of them. "Look on the floor."

One of the stone tiles protrudes a little higher than the rest of the floor. Verdan instructs them to put their backs against the walls. He steps on the tile, and it is pressed down into the floor. Suddenly a bunch of arrows flies across the center of the passageway, past the warriors. No one is harmed.

"Nice," Ramsay says.

They keep walking, turn right, and turn left into another stone passage.

"Wait," Verdan says.

He throws a ninja knife into the floor ahead and the tiles sag and crumble into a cavernous hole, with sharp spikes at the bottom. Once the dust has settled, the teams walk cautiously around the jagged edge of the hole and continue following Verdan. At the end of the passage is a large room with a stone golem in the center, sitting like an inanimate object. As they cross the threshold of the door, its eyes begin to glow, and it starts attacking them as it comes to life.

Ramsay blocks with his shield as the golem hits him with its heavy arms. Jonwido shoots dark energy balls at it, Eldon thrusts it with the spear, Romulus chops it with the axe, and Verdan swipes it with his knives. The golem soon falls to pieces on the floor. Ramsay's bruises are healed by Chase.

They walk across the room into another passageway, which takes them into an empty room.

"Could we have taken a wrong turn?" Chase wonders aloud.

"No, wait," Verdan says as he looks closely at the walls. "Aha!"

He moves towards one wall and strikes it. The illusion disappears and another passageway is revealed. The teams come to a fork in the path and decide to take the left way. They walk for a while but circle around back to the same fork.

"We were here before," Ramsay says.

"Let's go right this time," Irina says.

They take the path on the right, and it leads them into an open courtyard. Statues from a past civilization have succumbed to centuries of harsh weather and lie in moss-covered stone piles around their original plinths.

Something dark moves behind the debris. Six huge spiders come scuttling toward the group, low and fast across the ground. They are hairy and black with red stripes. Phinara screams at the sight. One springs at Ramsay, and he slices it in half with his sword. Another spider jumps on Verdan like a cricket, scrabbling on his body. He shakes it off him and slices it with his two knives.

"That was gross, eww," Verdan exclaims, wiping spider blood off his arm.

Romulus smashes a spider with his axe and Ramsay kills a few more of them. Eldon impales the last one on his spear like a shish kebab as it jumps at him.

Shuddering in disgust, they move through the court-yard. The stone door leading to the next room is closed. There are four square tiles on the ground in front of it with pictures of people on them. Verdan tests one of the tiles by compressing it. Nothing happens.

"Each of the tiles has an image of a person on it. Perhaps it takes four people to open it. Let's try having someone stand on each tile," Chase says.

Ramsay, Romulus, Eldon, and Phinara each choose a tile to stand on. The floor grumbles and the stone door slides open.

The warriors enter a large chamber. A round platform surrounded by metal rods is positioned at the far end. There is a metallic panel with levers on the side of it. As they approach the middle area, a hole opens in the ceiling, and a bulky creature with the head of a bull drops down with a crash. It has sizeable, hairy arms and holds a double-ended sword in its hand. The minotaur drops its head and aims its curved horns at the enemy.

It bellows at the trespassers and the battle commences. Verdan is struck down, but as his body falls onto the floor, it is substituted with a broken pillar. He stands unharmed on the other side of the room. Ramsay gets the minotaur's attention by banging his shield. He dodges a couple of slashes and counters with a few of his own. Chase puts a healing circle on the ground.

Jonwido fires electricity at the monster, but it turns and rushes at him with a swing. Jonwido receives a strike and backs away. Irina fires a barrage of arrows into its back. It turns and runs at her, but she rolls and dodges the attack. The minotaur's movements are quick and erratic.

Ramsay and Romulus try to get its attention, but it has set its sights on the healers. Jonwido has recovered slightly from the blow and gets into the fight again. He shoots the beast with electric attacks again, halting its motion slightly.

Eldon engages it, but his attacks are deflected. Ramsay and Romulus join Eldon, attacking the minotaur together from the front and back. Their combined effort is successful, and they finish it off as it falls to the stone floor.

"Good fighting everyone," Ramsay says breathlessly as they dust themselves off and regroup.

"That must be the teleporter," Chase says, walking toward the platform.

He walks to the control panel and pushes up one of the levers. Clunky sounds are heard as the machine activates. The platform lights up.

"I'm assuming that we just stand and wait on the platform now," Chase says.

"Yeah, and the piece of junk will teleport us *safely* to our destination," Verdan says, sarcastically.

"Only one way to find out," Ramsay says.

Chase steps onto the teleporter and disappears with a bright flash as he moves to the center. The others follow and are transferred one by one. Somewhere in the floating islands of Eivulth, the linked teleporter activates, and our warriors materialize onto it. It is almost identical to the one in the temple.

"I'm still me," Jonwido says, as he looks at his hands.

"That felt weird. It's like a sleepy foot, except it's my whole body," Verdan says.

"It's not that bad," Eldon says, as he finds his balance.

"Says the dragon slayer!" Verdan says, teasingly.

Everyone teleports successfully. They gather and try to make sense of where they are. It is obvious that they're not in a temple anymore. It looks like a craggy, mountainous area with trees and bushes. However, they are in the sky and clouds surround the island. Other floating islands can be seen in the distance, like giant icebergs made from rock drifting in the sky.

"We've arrived in Eivulth," Chase says with relief.

"How are the islands not falling?" Ramsay asks.

"I'm not sure. It's probably some kind of magnetic phenomenon or a powerful incantation. It's been like this since prehistoric times," Chase says.

As the group proceeds, an enormous mountain shaped like a table comes into view. At the summit, many dragons are flying like bats.

"The alpha's lair is probably in that mountain," Chase says.

They stop in their tracks as two dragons land near them. Eldon and Ramsay run in front, getting ready for battle. Phinara starts putting up a dome shield as the others spread out.

"Halt! We mean you no harm," the black dragon says.

"There is no need for violence," The green dragon says.

Ramsay and the team lower their weapons.

"Why? The other dragons we came across attacked us without hesitation," Ramsay asks.

"We have not been assigned to torment men."

"Many of us do not agree with the cruel wishes of our Lord, but we cannot disobey once an order has been given. Why have you come to this place?"

"We have come here to slay your king. This is our mission. We cannot allow our people to be attacked by dragons again. Are you going to stop us?" Ramsay says.

The dragons look at each other for a moment.

"If our king is defeated, that would be liberating indeed. I do not understand how eight people would be able to do it, but we can take you to his lair. However, we cannot assist you in your battle, because we are completely vulnerable to his control," the black dragon says.

"That would be of great help. We'd appreciate it." Ramsay says.

"Can it be that some of the dragons are good?" Eldon asks, turning to Chase.

"Should we trust them?" Jonwido asks.

"Well, if they wanted us dead, we'd be on fire by now," Chase says.

"My name is Kosynth. Climb on, and grip your possessions," the black dragon says.

"I am Tugerre," the green dragon says.

The dragons fetch another one of their kin, Bytu, to transport Ramsay's party. Irina and Ramsay ride on Kosynth's back, while Tugerre and Bytu carry three people each. As they increase in altitude, they get a spectacular view of the world beneath. Below them are the floating islands, and further down is the land of Yragos, partially obscured by the clouds.

"Get me down! It's too high!" Jonwido shouts with his eyes shut as he desperately clutches the dragon.

"Woohoo!" Eldon shouts, enjoying the ride.

"Awesome," Ramsay says, with Irina's arms around his waist.

"What an experience," Phinara exclaims.

None of the warriors have ridden a flying mount before. They hold on tightly as the powerful beasts cut through the wind.

The dragons drop them off at a concealed entrance to a cave on the side of the great mountain. The warriors are wide awake with adrenaline.

"This cave shall lead you to the Lord. Tread lightly and you may find him sleeping," the green dragon says.

The party walks into the cave and follows the winding tunnel. There are glowing crystals sticking out of the walls.

Some of them are blue and some green. Reaching the end of the tunnel, they enter a massive cavern and discover the alpha dragon coiled up in his nest. Multi-colored scales cover his long dark grey body. A few holes in the ceiling allow sunbeams to shine through. The light creates rainbow colours on the dragon in much the same way it does in a puddle of oil. Two large arms are attached to the upper part of its serpentine body.

The teams move forward slowly and try to remain undetected while assessing the situation. The sound of the alpha's breathing vibrates through the cavern.

"He looks like he's sleeping. What do we do?" Eldon whispers.

"I'll use the dragon orb as soon as I can. If things go sour, try to distract him as much as possible," Ramsay says quietly.

"Look at the size of him. That is sheer power," Romulus whispers.

Verdan accidentally kicks a rock over the edge, and the noise rings through the cavern as it hits the rocks at the bottom floor. This snaps the alpha dragon out of its restful state, and it notices the intruders. At first, he mistakes them for animals but quickly realizes that they are men.

"Who dares to enter my lair?" the alpha says with a thunderous voice.

"This ends today dragon! You're not going to cause

any more suffering! Prepare to die!" Ramsay shouts.

"Bwahahaha!" the alpha laughs. "How amusing...let me see what you can do before I devour you all."

Ramsay nods at the rest of the team and runs to a ledge closer to the alpha. The others draw their weapons and get into position. Chase boosts Ramsay's defense as usual. Ramsay then takes out the dragon shackle orb and points it at the alpha. It shines brightly as he begins reciting the incantation.

"I know what that is. Not so fast!"

The alpha lifts himself up and starts moving around. The dragon orb flickers on and off.

"We need to bind him!" Ramsay shouts.

Chase and Phinara start casting their most powerful binding spells. The alpha targets Ramsay, rushing at him with bared teeth. Ramsay jumps out of the way, rolling and dropping the orb. He quickly runs after it. Jonwido casts a huge ice spell and throws sharp icicles at the alpha, embedding them into its body. It roars and looks around.

Irina darts into view and tries to distract him by firing electric arrows. An arrow flies into one of the alpha's eyes. Blood squirts out of his eye as he shakes his head. He turns his attention to Irina, launching himself at her. She screams as he pierces her through the chest with his powerful claw. The alpha flings her aside and she falls to the ground like a rag doll.

"Irina! No!" Ramsay shouts in horror.

"She's gone! You must finish the incantation!" Chase shouts to Ramsay.

"We'll bind him!" Phinara shouts.

Giant chains of light form around the alpha's body as Chase finishes casting his spell. Phinara also finishes her spell and an enormous magic circle appears over the dragon. He falls, pinned to the ground with great force, unable to move. Eldon and Romulus guard Chase and Phinara as they hold their hands up.

"Now Ramsay! Now!" Chase shouts.

Ramsay holds the orb up and starts the incantation again. The orb shines brightly as Ramsay completes it, and the alpha's energy flows into the orb like a whirlwind. The alpha roars and curses as it is weakened. The damage dealers then combine their attacks against the incapacitated king, finishing him off.

"Yes! Well done!" Chase shouts.

Everyone cheers. Ramsay holds the shackle orb in his hands as it radiates. He's hardly able to look at it.

"It's time to make a wish, man," Eldon says as he stands by Ramsay.

"I was going to use the wish to bring back those who died in Nashia," Ramsay says as he looks at Irina's body.

Verdan, Romulus, and Phinara are standing by their

dead comrade. Phinara is crying while the others stare at the ground.

"I've always put the mission first, and tried to help those in need, but this time I'm going to do something for myself," Ramsay says, as a tear rolls down his cheek.

"I wish to resurrect Irina!" Ramsay says as he points the orb in Irina's direction.

Energy flows out of the orb and into Irina's body. Suddenly she is enveloped in a white light, and her wounds are healed. Her eyes slowly open and she wakes up, looking down at her ripped and blood-soaked clothes. The dragon shackle orb deactivates and becomes a dull grey color.

"I remember being attacked by the dragon. What happened?"

"You were dead!" Phinara says, running to hug her. "Ramsay's wish brought you back to life."

"What have you done? That wish could've been used for anything." Chase says with criticism.

Ramsay stares silently at Chase for a moment, as if facing his darkest fear, but he realizes that he made the right decision. Irina lifts her head weakly to gaze across at the dead alpha dragon. With Phinara's help, she gets slowly to her feet and walks to Ramsay.

"Thank you," Irina says as Ramsay smiles at her.

"You've made me happy, and I just couldn't bear the thought of losing you here," Ramsay says.

"I'm glad you feel the same way," Irina says and they embrace each other.

A multitude of dragons roar in the distance. More roars come from deeper inside the cave.

"Oh shit, they're coming," Jonwido says.

"The other dragons must have sensed that their king has been slain. We must get out of here," Chase says.

The team hurries back the way they came in. Outside the cave, a horde of flying dragons blacken the sky above them. The warriors flee on a trail down the mountain. Dragons who were loyal to the alpha catch sight of them and begin pursuing them.

"They're on our tail!" Ramsay shouts.

"At this rate..." Chase says and trails off.

"Guys! I'll protect you!" Jonwido shouts while running with the group.

They glance at him.

"This is my chance to be the hero for a change. I can't watch you guys die. You're the only family I have left!"

"What? No! Jon!" Ramsay shouts.

Jonwido stops and turns around to face the horde of dragons. He fires huge thunderbolts upwards to catch their attention. As they circle him and get closer, he uses all the energy he has left to cast one last spell. His eyes glow as he creates a gigantic mass of ice around himself, catching all the dragons that were pursuing his team.

Alas, his body is frozen in the icy tomb as well.

Shocked and subdued, the team sits near Jon's body among the debris of ice and frozen dragons wondering how to proceed. After a while, a lone shadow drifts overhead and to their relief, it's Kosynth, who lands beside them and offers to carry the fleeing party to safety. Ramsay mounts Kosynth, and the rest of the team is carried by Tugerre and Bytu all the way to Yragos. They land near the town of Kine, away from any people to avoid frightening them. No hostile dragons are following behind.

"Dammit! We lost Jon!" Ramsay says as he stomps the ground.

"He sacrificed himself so that we could escape. He was a true hero," Eldon says.

"Yes..." Chase says solemnly.

"I'm sorry for your team's loss," Irina says.

"Thank you, warriors. You have done us a great service," Kosynth says.

"The dragons of Eivulth are confused now. We have no leader," Tugerre says.

"Most of us will return to our world until there is a new alpha. Your kind will have peace for a long time," Bytu says.

"I hope so, but we have a way of finding new trouble. Wait here, please. We will fetch a friend and come back," Ramsay says.

Ramsay, Eldon, and Chase go into town to fetch Peakiboon and find him sleeping in a barn.

"Hey Peakiboon, we're back," Ramsay says.

"Hey! Ramsay and Eldon! You made it!" Peakiboon says.

"Do you want to come with us?"

"Yep. Let's go. I was getting bored here."

After returning to the dragons with Peakiboon, they fly all the way to Ilaburn and land on a hill outside the city. The sun is beginning to set.

"Wheee! That was cool!" Peakiboon exclaims.

"It would be wise for you to leave us here, and return to Eivulth," Chase says to the dragons.

"Yes, we shall take our leave now. Goodbye, warriors," Kosynth says.

The three dragons fly away, glad that they are finally free of their vengeful leader. Their silhouettes fade off into the sky.

Ramsay and the team spend the night at Ilaburn, recovering from their ordeal.

Today they have been pushed to their limits, both physically and emotionally.

CHAPTER 9

TREASURE FOR A LIFETIME

The great mission has been completed, and all that's left for the teams is to return to Nashia with the good news. The friends set out together early in the morning. They no longer feel like separate teams. Journeying through the desert and the forest, they arrive at the city of Nashia.

This lively city, their home, is safe again. They are greeted by the sentries at the main gate as they walk in. The blood on their armor and garments makes them look more valorous than usual. The group is congratulated and cheered as they walk down the streets. Ramsay receives many high-fives from acquaintances. The heroes, weary from the journey, head to the warrior's guild to report on what happened.

They meet with the guildmaster.

"The dragon alpha has been defeated. We made use of the dragon shackle orb provided by the legendary Galather. Our team worked together with Team Pandeaqead to achieve this," Chase says, nodding at Irina's team.

"Marvelous. Where is your comrade, Jonwido?" Seth asks.

"He has been killed in battle, sir," Ramsay answers.

"How unfortunate. He died with honor, and we will see to it that he has a proper memorial service," Seth says.

"Thank you, guildmaster," Eldon says.

"What of the talking rabbit?" Seth asks.

"He has assisted us on our mission," Ramsay says.

"Oh, congratulations rabbit. You will be awarded for bravery," Seth says.

"Peakiboon enjoys killing monsters. Yep."

"I thank you again, warriors. Your names will go down in the history books, and you can look forward to your reward."

"One more thing, sir," Ramsay says.

"Speak."

"I've decided to resign from the warriors' guild."

"That's a surprise. Your talents will surely be missed."

"What? You're quitting?" Eldon asks, in shock.

"Sir, me too," Irina says.

"Aye, Miss Irina. Thank you for your service. You've been a powerful role model."

The teams leave the guildmaster's office and walk outside.

"I know it's unexpected, but I've thought about it a lot. Irina and I have decided to leave the guild and start a family together. It would be best if I'm not out on missions all the time. One could retire with the amount of gold we'll be receiving from the king. I think I'll do some farming to keep myself busy," Ramsay explains.

"Haha, I can't imagine you as a farmer," Eldon says as he chuckles.

"Wow, you're leaving us?" Verdan expresses amazement as he turns to Irina.

"Yeah guys, it's been fun. I'll miss you. We can still hang out sometimes." Irina says as she hugs her former teammates.

"What are your plans?" Ramsay asks Chase, as they consider their futures.

"I will focus on research, and document what I've discovered about the dragons. The technology used in the teleportation devices was also quite interesting," Chase says.

A FEW DAYS LATER, the king orders that a grand feast is held to commemorate the defeat of the dragon alpha and honor the victorious warriors. He rewards them each with land and a chest of gold. At the feast, the king makes a speech, informing everyone that the dragon threat has been stopped.

Ramsay and his comrades are praised, and a large image of Jonwido is put on display, with flowers and candles. The decorations do not match the black clothing and dark expression he wears in his picture, but his friends will remember the kind of man he was. After the speech, the servants bring out the food and drinks and all the smartly dressed guests have a good time.

Galather walks up to Ramsay and starts a conversation. His outfit is impressive, with fancy embroidery on his robe. Chase excuses himself and joins his female companion.

"Hi, Master Galather. It's good to see you again," Ramsay says.

"It's good to see that you're back in Nashia, alive and kicking."

"It's all thanks to you. The orb worked in the end. I'll return it to you soon."

"You were the right man for the task. You've overcome every obstacle in your way and made the right choices. I see you've also found love. That's what it's all about. I'm very proud of you." Galather says, smiling.

"Thanks, Master," Ramsay says, smiling.

The music begins playing, and Ramsay and Irina move towards the dance floor, hand-in-hand.

"I told you we'd win," Irina says, as they face each other, and she draws him closer.

"Yes, you were right," Ramsay says.

MEANWHILE, in a certain jungle, warriors of Nashia sit on benches, blissfully eating fruit.

"Pass me some more of the delicious fruit, barbarian," Danjurou says.

"Yes, yes, eat as much as you want. You are our honored guests," Irkal says with a smirk.

"How long have we been here?" one of Danjurou's teammates asks.

"No need to stress. There is enough time for us to spoil ourselves before defeating the dragon."

Gatthuta brings them some jugs of juice. The samurai drinks and begins singing merrily with his team...

Two years later...

Eldon walks into the final room of a dungeon with his team. A ferocious demon beast appears, roaring and shooting lighting out of its head. The mage positions himself and gets ready to heal his party. The tank rushes ahead to face it. Eldon sprints and jumps over the beast, landing at its rear. He attacks it with a combo of thrusts, swipes, and stabs. After a fierce battle, the boss is defeated, and the team claims the treasure that they came for.

"Damn, you can jump pretty high," Arnor says, as he sheathes his sword.

"Yeah, I eat ten grasshoppers every morning," Eldon says and chuckles.

Meanwhile, in the temple of Acohr, Chase examines the parts of the teleporter closely. He is assisted by a team of specialists who use technical equipment to analyze the device.

"This is definitely Zeosine technology."

A man stands squinting at the symbols on one of the walls, comparing them with information in a book he's holding. The teleporter is started up, and a couple of researchers step into it. They vanish and reappear at the floating islands of Eivulth. After taking a moment to recover, they observe the situation there. Kosynth and Tugerre descend, creating a gust of wind as they flap their wings. They approach the researchers to greet them. However, the men scream and flee to the teleporter, sending themselves back to the temple.

"They do not know that all the wild ones have left," Kosynth says.

<hr>

MEANWHILE, on a farm somewhere in Nashia, Ramsay and Irina sit in their home, having breakfast.

"How are the crops doing?" Irina asks.

"The corn is almost ready for harvest. They're growing well."

The baby starts crying, and Irina gets up to check on him. Ramsay finishes his breakfast and gets ready to go out. The sword he used when facing the alpha dragon is mounted against the wall in the living room. Irina's bow is mounted on the adjacent wall.

"Have a good day honey, I'm going out to see if all the sheep have been sheared."

"Okay, see you later. I'll make some of those muffins you like."

Ramsay opens the wooden door and steps outside. He stretches and takes a deep breath of fresh air on the porch.

Rebel is tied to a post nearby. He neighs as Ramsay walks past. On the way to the sheep pen, Peakiboon hops out of a nearby barn.

"Hey, Peakiboon. I'm on my way to check the sheep shearing. Wanna join me?"

From the kitchen window, Irina smiles as she watches the companionable pair head down the path to the shearing shed.

The worker is busy shearing the last sheep when Ramsay arrives. Sacks of raw wool are set down neatly in a row. As they greet, a wolf is heard howling. The sheep bleat and scramble with fear, as the huge beast approaches the pen. Ramsay quickly reaches out and grabs a pitchfork. He has a stare-down with the wolf, then coats himself with a defensive spell, and charges forward valiantly with the pitchfork.

You've completed the adventure!

Thanks for the support.
I'd really appreciate it if you posted a review!

About the Author

Caleb Birch has a BTech in Electrical Engineering and several years of experience in Embedded Software Development. He is passionate about all things philosophical and applies critical thinking to discover truth. When he is not writing code, he is writing fantasy. Caleb also enjoys spending hours playing video games.

For more information about this book and the upcoming sequel, please visit:

www.fantasymission.co.za

Updates will also be shared on instagram:
@caleb_b111

www.ingramcontent.com/pod-product-compliance
Lightning Source LLC
Chambersburg PA
CBHW031336060726
47590CB00007B/2488